GRANNY'S JUSTICE

GRANNY'S JUSTICE

James Campbell

JaMar

GRANNY'S JUSTICE

Copyright 2013 by James Campbell

ISBN: 978-0-615-75035-4

Printed and bound in the United States of America. All rights reserved. No part of this book may be reproduced in any form or by any electronic or mechanical means including information storage and retrieval system without permission in writing from the copyright holder.

Published by

JaMar Publishing

6635 Baptist Valley Rd.
North Tazewell, VA 24630

Tel: 276 988-9504

E-mail: jtcampsr@netscope.net
Web: www.jamescampbellbooks.com

All the characters in this book have no existence outside the imagination of the author and have no relation whatsoever to anyone bearing the same name or names. Any individual known or unknown does not inspire them to the author, and all incidents are pure invention.

Other books by James Campbell

Luther's Mule

Ida Mae: Moonshine, Money & Misery

In Her Sister's Shadow

INTRODUCTION

Rosa Lee, the matriarch of the Duncan family, had performed her duties well since the death of her husband. But, as the number of descendents increased, so did the responsibility of overseeing their welfare. Although the younger generation did not often seek her advice or follow it when it was given, when a disaster arose no one questioned her ability to take matters in hand.

It was high noon the day after Thanksgiving and only one day past the Duncan family's second reunion. It was a time that should have been filled with exciting memories of the previous day's festivities, but those memories were overshadowed by what lay ahead.

Ira, head of the Duncan household and newly appointed Sheriff of the county, sat with his wife, Mary Ellen, on the front porch of the home they would be leaving before the end of the week Kervin and Kevin, their twin boys, were seated just below on a large flat stone that served as the first step to the two-story farmhouse.

Ira was slowly increasing the size of a pile of shavings that lay between his feet as he whittled away on a piece of cedar. Mary Ellen was mending a hole in the heel of a stocking that should have been disposed of three washings before, and the twins took turns shooting pebbles at a Prince Albert tobacco can they'd nailed to the yard gate post. Although they seemed intent on what they were doing, they each knew what was on the other's mind. It was a small single story dwelling that stood on a knoll about half-mile away. The house was tiny compared to where they now lived, but it was where they would soon call home.

Chapter One

RECALLING OLD MEMORIES

It was only an hour past sun down, but it might just as well been midnight because the down pouring rain and the dense fog made it almost impossible to see. Jake Hurd and his wife, Ida Mae, were feeling their way down the mountain just north of the North Carolina state line. Ida Mae's sister, Mary Sue, and their grandmother Rosa Lee were passengers in the back seat. Moments earlier they had been having an enjoyable conversation about the events of the previous day, but suddenly their safety had become their primary concern. The visibility was barely past the hood ornament of his Ninety-Eight Olds, and everyone's nerves were strained to the max. Jake was giving his full attention to what might lie ahead, and the ladies were on the edge of their seat. Mary Sue was gripping the door handle so tightly her knuckles were white.

Suddenly, from out of nowhere, the tail lights of a semi came into view. Jake slammed on the brakes, sending the Oldsmobile into a tailspin. When at last their automobile came to a halt, everyone breathed a sigh of relief. Mary Sue leaned forward, face in hands, and stammered, "Boy, that was close." Ida Mae patted Jake's trembling leg and congratulated him on his driving ability. Granny pulled herself up out of the floor, brushed her hair from her eyes, and asked Jake if he would kindly find a safe parking place so she could locate her dentures. Her comment brought a chuckle from the others and relieved the tension for the moment.

"Gladly," he answered. "We'd better get off this highway until the fog lifts, or we might all get killed. Aren't we near that little diner, the one you told me about, Mom's Place To Eat or something or other?"

"Mama's Home Cooking," Ida Mae reminded him.

"That's it. We'll stop there for a while if I can find the place in all this fog." Jake drove back onto the highway; in less than a minute, the neon lights over the door of the diner came into view.

"Got 'em," Granny chirped as she blew hard upon her uppers and placed them back in her mouth.

"We'll sit here for a spell until the rain lets up and then have a bite to eat," Jake suggested.

"Not me," Granny blurted. "I need at least two cups of strong coffee to settle my nerves."

Ida Mae smiled as she watched her grandmother splashing through the deep puddles toward the entrance to the diner.

Rosa Lee was spry for a lady in her sixties and time had done little to take away from her good looks or her feisty behavior. As a matter of fact, she was the envy of most of the women who were members of her Ladies Quilting Bee. She had been a widow for several years and quite often made comments about finding herself a good looking rich feller. When anyone in the family teased her about it, she assured them she was only kidding, but everyone knew she'd had her sights set on Brother Taylor, who had passed on before she could get him to the altar. Living with her only child, Ira Duncan, the recently appointed sheriff of Russell County, gave her a feeling of security, but was not how she planned to spend her sunset years.

Jake and the ladies remained in the shelter of the car for another half-hour until at last there was a break in the storm. As soon as it seemed they would not get drowned, they made a mad dash for the diner. The threesome welcomed the warmth of the dining area and the country music playing on the jukebox. Jake scanned the premises for the whereabouts of their companion but did not see her right away. He moved closer to the bar and gave his eyes a moment to adjust to the dim lighting.

"Over here!" someone called.

Jake recognized Rose Lee's voice. She was seated at a half-circle booth in one corner of the dining room. Across from her was a well-dressed gentleman who seemed to be enjoying her company. The fellow came to his feet as Jake, Ida Mae and Mary Sue reached their table.

"This is Randolph Patrick, young'uns. He offered to share his table since the place is so crowded. I reckon the storm made all these folks want to get off the highway. Anyway, Randolph, like myself, lost his companion a few years back so he's been living alone on a large farm up in Bland County. He has lots of shares in a tobacco company down in North Carolina and has interest in an automobile dealership. That's his Caddy parked outside, the new blue one with the dealer tag."

It was all Jake could do to keep from laughing. He was amazed at how much Granny had learned about this stranger in such a short time. He was even more amazed at how willing this fellow had been to share so much about his personal life with someone he had just met.

"These are my granddaughters, Ida Mae and Mary Sue; and this young man is Jake Hurd, Ida Mae's husband."

Randolph shook hands with each of them. "Please have a seat; this booth is rather small so I'll sit somewhere else so you won't be crowded."

"Nonsense," Rosa Lee insisted. "We don't mind being a little crowded. Besides there's not another seat in the house."

"Okay. Just until this fog lifts, and then I must be going."

"Randolph goes down to Mt. Airy every weekend to visit his son. Stops here on Friday evening for supper. He says they make the best chicken and dumplings in the whole state. We'll have to try them sometime."

Again, Jake chuckled to himself, amazed at how much Rosa Lee had learned about this fellow. Randolph squeezed back into the booth beside her just as a uniformed officer entered the restaurant.

"May I have your attention?" He spoke in a rather loud voice. "There has been a huge mud-slide halfway down the mountain near the state line, and the highway is blocked in both directions. If you are not headed north or live nearby, you might just as well settle in for the night. You will stay open for these travelers, won't you, Magdalene?" The comment was directed at the proprietor behind the counter whom he knew quite well.

Rosa Lee picked up a menu that lay in front of her. "Then I guess we should order some of those chicken and dumplings right now and learn more about each other," she suggested.

Jake hid his face behind his menu, leaned close to Ida Mae and whispered, "I thought Granny knew everything there was to know already."

She gave him a light kick under the table and smiled. "You're right," she said, pretending to be replying to her granny's comment.

"Friday's special for everyone, Irene; and it's my treat," Randolph told the waitress the next time she passed their booth. "Now where were we?"

"I believe Granny was about to find out his blood type," Jake whispered once more.

This time the kick was a little more brisk.

The small, newly acquainted party spent the next few hours drinking coffee and listening to the jukebox. Sometime past midnight, someone suggested they return to their automobiles and try to catch a few winks.

"But I'm not sleepy," Granny offered.

"You will be come daybreak, and it will beat sitting here in this booth the rest of the night," Ida Mae warned.

"Let's you and me sleep in my car and the girls will have more room in your Olds," Randolph suggested. "We can all get together in the morning, say seven-thirty, and have breakfast."

After hearing these arrangements, Granny agreed to retire for a little shuteye.

The downpour had diminished to a slow, cold, sprinkle making it a little less dreadful reaching their respective automobiles. Jake watched until the ladies were safe inside his car then slid into the passenger's seat of Patrick's sky-blue Cadillac. The cold leather seat contacting his damp clothing sent a chill through his body. Randolph started the engine of his luxury machine; and in a few moments, the interior was as warm and cozy as could be. He lowered the rear windows about half-inch to reduce the risk of being overcome by carbon monoxide. "Make yourself as comfortable as possible," he instructed Jake as he moved the driver's seat backwards and reclined it full length. Jake followed suit. The last thing he remembered was the sound of soft music from the radio, the warmth of the heater and the smell of new paint.

Sleep did not come as rapidly for the ladies, however. As soon as they were settled in, Granny began talking about what a wonderful gentleman Randolph was.

"I thought you were going to North Carolina to see your old boyfriend, Granny," Mary Sue teased. "How come you and old what's-his-name never got hitched?"

"His name is Sidney, and it's like this," Rosa Lee began. "I was born and grew up on a small farm near the mouth of Wilder Hollow somewhere south of where we now live, but you girls knew that already. The farm was passed on to my daddy, Theodore Wilcox, better known as Teddy, when his parents died. According to Daddy, the farm was so small and the soil of such poor quality it would grow little more than rabbits and blackberry briers. Most folks who lived around Wilder Hollow knew better but that was the best excuse my daddy could think of to find employment away from home. Some of the neighbors thought Mother convinced him to settle down before he was through sowing his wild oats which left him with the desire to spend lots of time away from home.

"But, be that as it may, throughout my growing up years, he worked in logging camps somewhere in and around Mingo County, West Virginia. He'd walk to the nearest train station, about three miles from home, the first day of each month and we wouldn't see him again for weeks. He, like many other lumberjacks, lived in the logging camps all but the last five days of each month at which time they came home to their families. The timber business was hard work but the pay was good and it was somewhat less dangerous than mining coal, which was the only other job at that time that paid well.

"Daddy's homecoming at month's end was a special time. He almost always got home late at night, lugging a small grip filled with soiled clothing; but somewhere tucked inside, he'd have a surprise for me. The following day he, Mom and I would walk to Davis's General Store to purchase enough supplies to last until his next trip home.

"Elbert Duff, another gentleman who lived some distance further up Wilder Hollow, also worked in Mingo County and traveled with my daddy. He, like Daddy, traveled light, but he did carry a much larger suitcase. It was no secret the extra space was needed for a moderate supply of moonshine he took back to camp each month. He never failed to explain it was scarcely enough for him and his buddies to have a toddy before their evening meal.

"Anyway, Elbert and his wife, like my parents, had only one child, a boy whom they named Sidney. He was a year or so older than I, but we attended the same elementary school. Each morning he came by our house, and we walked to class together. My mom liked Sidney a lot. She and Mrs. Duff were friends, and it was comforting for her to know I had someone to look after me. I thought he was okay, but I didn't share my mother's feelings until years later. In those early days, I thought he was over ambitious, always talking about wanting to be a lawyer or some highfaluting character like that. It was well known he made the highest marks in class and being the best looking young man in our vicinity added even more to his popularity.

"About the time he entered his junior year in high school, news about the invention of the Model-T Ford was headlines in every newspaper and magazine in the country. The first time Sidney saw a picture of this marvelous machine in the *Saturday Evening Post* he decided he had to have one. The fact that the price was $850 did nothing to lessen his determination. He began daydreaming about being the youngest man in Russell County to own one of these new black horseless carriages.

"When classes were over for the semester, he started working for anyone who needed help at whatever amount they were willing to pay; and to say he was frugal would be an understatement. By the end of summer, he had managed to save a mere eighty dollars. So, he dropped out of school shortly before the beginning of his senior year and went to work in the logging camps with his daddy. After a couple months of twelve-hour days of backbreaking labor, he decided he wanted no more of that.

"He did, however, enjoy partaking of the before dinner refreshments. That's when he decided that furnishing the logging camps with a larger amount of the relaxing liquid would be much more profitable and less strenuous than toiling all day in the timber business.

"There were over fifty men doing the timber cutting in addition to the sawmill workers and the crew that cared for the many teams of logging horses. He knew it would be much too risky to ship large amounts at one time, so he decided the alternative would be to make weekly trips from Wilder Hollow to Mingo County. So, despite his father's objections, he quit his job and began telling folks he had gotten employment with the railroad.

"By that time, I was in my mid-teens and was beginning to think about getting married and having a family of my own. The resentment I once had for Sidney's over ambition slowly turned into admiration. Before I knew it, I was in love. I was so naive and so overwhelmed by the money he was making, I believed he really was working for the Norfolk and Western Railway Company.

"He came courting every other Saturday evening. Many times Mother would sit on the front porch with the two of us and listen to him tell about the places the three of us would visit once he made enough money to purchase his Model-T. He had us so excited about our travels we begin counting the number of paydays before he could purchase the automobile.

"Daddy never mentioned anything about Sidney's whiskey-running business into Mingo County and little about anything else that took place in the logging camps. After all, he and Elbert were good friends; and he, too, enjoyed the refreshments his son made available to the loggers; therefore, he saw no need to discuss the matter. Likewise, Mother and I said little about the time Sidney and I was spending together.

"Everything went well for the first few weeks, and Sidney's net worth was increasing with each trip he made to the logging camps. He hinted that he would soon ask Daddy for permission for us to get married; and the more we spoke of these plans, the more impatient he became. It was his impatience that proved to be his downfall. He decided that if he expanded his business into other counties he could achieve his goal much faster.

"Logan County appeared to be the best choice geographically and would add little to his travels. He started shipping small wooden crates each week in addition to what he normally carried in his suitcase. The shipping charge was offset by the increase in profit so he was beginning to establish a very lucrative business. What he did not know was that a well-known family of whiskey makers already provided more than an ample amount of liquid refreshments to meet the demands in Logan County. He was soon to learn they did not intend to allow an outsider to horn in on their business. So to eliminate his intrusion, they secretly told the railroad detectives what he was doing.

"During one of his trips to Logan County, he discovered he was in trouble. He boarded the passenger car as usual, carefully placed the whiskey filled suitcase in the overhead compartment as he had done every time before. Later that evening when he returned from the dining car, he discovered his suitcase was missing. In a few minutes a tall, broad-shouldered, muscular gentleman wearing an expensive suit sat in the seat across the isle from him. 'Know who owns the grip that was stored overhead?' he asked.

"'No Sir.'

"'Suppose you don't know anything about some crates being delivered to the freight station in Mingo County either, right?'

"'That's right, Sir.'

"Sidney denied the case or the crate belonged to him, and when questioned further, swore he had no knowledge of what was inside.

"I remember well the very last time I saw him," she continued. "He and I were sitting on the front porch of my house waiting for our Dads to come home. He appeared to be troubled, and I suspected it was because of what he thought the answer might be when he asked for permission for us to marry. I was to discover soon that was not the case at all; for shortly before time for his arrival, two neatly dressed men came into view a ways down the path leading to our house. Suddenly Sidney became as nervous as a long-tailed cat in a room full of rocking chairs.

"'If they're railroad detectives tell them you haven't seen me. I promise I'll be back for you when I get my Model-T.'

"These were his final words just before he leaped from our porch into history. Days became weeks without a word from him. I didn't learn the true story about his sudden departure until more than a month after he was gone. Within a couple days, Sidney's parents also left the county in order to avoid having to explain their son's illegal activities.

"I was nearing my seventeenth birthday and I was so angry, hurt and disappointed I just wanted to some how get even. Two months later, I married your grandfather Buford. Although I was very fond of him, I wondered if I had made the right choice, but by that time I was expecting your father. You girls know the rest of the story."

Just past daybreak the next morning, Jake was awakened by the sound of loud snoring. The rain had stopped; the fog was beginning to lift; the car engine was no longer running, and there was a brisk chill in the air. The flashing neon sign over the restaurant door made him realize where he was. He moved his seat to the upright position just in time to see Rosa Lee make her way inside.

"Are you hungry, Jake?" It was Randolph who must have been disturbed when he began moving.

"No, but coffee would hit the spot. Why don't you go on in, and I'll check on the ladies?" Jake walked to his car and saw that his wife and sister-in-law were still sleeping like babies. He couldn't resist, he quietly unlocked the door on the driver's side and mashed down hard on the horn button causing both ladies to almost jump out of their seats.

Ida Mae quickly sat upright, surveyed her surroundings, "Where's Granny?" she asked.

"Oh, she's been inside for sometime, probably helping get Randolph's breakfast," Jake laughed.

They made their way inside and took turns freshening up while waiting to be served. Just as they finished eating, another police officer came in to tell everyone that one lane of the highway was now unblocked and could be used, but to use with extreme caution. "Not until we have another cup of coffee," Rosa Lee suggested. After having her cup filled the third time, it became evident she was in no hurry to leave; but Ida Mae insisted they must go.

"It has been great meeting you and spending time together," Randolph told Rosa Lee as they made their exit. "Sure hope to see you again. Remember, I'm here every Friday evening."

Rosa Lee's smile was all the assurance he needed that he would see her again.

Granny didn't mention Randolph any time during the remainder of their trip, but everyone knew how infatuated she was.

Chapter Two

GRANNY GETS HOMESICK

Half-hour after leaving the diner, they were crossing the state line into North Carolina. A short time later, the Mt. Airy city limit sign came into view.

"Want to stop and try to find your old beau?" Ida Mae asked jokingly.

"Not on your life," Granny snarled. "I don't even want that old boy to know I'm still living until I'm ready."

"Shucks, if you and Randolph get to see each other another time or two you might completely forget about Sidney," Ida Mae continued to tease. "Where does he live any way?"

"Son-of-a-gun," Granny gasped. "Can you believe I forgot to ask?"

"I sure can't," the words were out of Jake's mouth before he could bridle his tongue.

Ida Mae winked at him and rapidly changed the subject. In another couple hours, they were back home on Chestnut Street in Winston Salem.

Granny spent the next few days pretending to be happy taking in the sights of the city, but her granddaughters knew this was not the case. On occasion, she talked about how nice Randolph was and that she would like to get to know him better. Other times she was making plans to rekindle the flame that once burned for Sidney. But, her phone calls back home had become more frequent so the girls knew she was becoming homesick. Not only was she missing her family members back in the mountains, she was concerned for their safety.

Ira kept reassuring his mother that the moonshine runners had turned to other methods of making a living, but Rosa Lee's concern for her son's well being was foremost in her thoughts. She was not totally convinced that Baxter, the former sheriff, was willing to let his resentment toward the Duncan family rest without retaliation.

It was Mary Ellen who at last persuaded her to enjoy her time with her granddaughters and take advantage of life in the city.

Once she was satisfied that all was well back home, she begin dwelling on her plans to continue her investigation into the life of her old beau.

Her intentions were to go up to Mt. Airy and find out as much as she could about the Judge without his knowing she was there. The girls made lots of suggestions but none seemed to appeal to her. Jake's suggestion that she go to Mt. Airy, change her name, rob a bank and surprise Old Sidney when she came to trial didn't appeal to Granny either, but it sparked a new set of ideas. The next morning she was out of bed early. As soon as breakfast was finished, she asked Ida Mae to take her shopping.

"Any place in particular?" she asked.

"Wherever I can purchase these items," Granny said, handing a shopping list to her granddaughter.

Ida Mae read from the list: one dark wig, one new hat, and a pair of dark rimmed glasses. She folded the small piece of paper and gave it back to Granny. "You got it," she smiled, "I know just the place." The three ladies headed downtown; and before the morning ended, Granny had the items she needed to assure she would not be recognized.

"Now, reckon you might take me to Mt. Airy sometime?" she asked.

"Tomorrow morning soon enough?"

Granny smiled and nodded.

By noon the following day Ida Mae, Mary Sue and Rosa Lee were in Mt. Airy. Rosa Lee was determined to learn as much about her old beau as possible before deciding if she wanted to renew their friendship. To do so would require a bit of detective work. What she did not know was that her granddaughter had already learned a bit of useful information the evening before.

When they got into town Ida Mae drove straight to the parking lot adjacent to the law offices of Smith, Donnelly and Wallace. "Come along, Granny. Let's go plead your case."

Rosa Lee looked puzzled but made no comment. They entered the attorney's office and walked to a desk where a young female receptionist was typing at full speed. As soon as she was aware of their presence, she stopped what she was doing.

"Good day, ladies. No use taking a seat; Mr. Wallace is expecting you. This way please. How are things with you Mary Sue?" she added.

Mary Sue gave the thumbs-up signal indicating that all was well.

"Bill Wallace is the attorney who kept Mary Sue and J. D. off the gallows," Ida Mae whispered to Granny as they followed the young lady down the hallway. "His sister-in-law's parents lived with Jake and me while his brother was in the hospital. Never hurts to have a member of the bar on your side, especially when you plan to investigate a Circuit Court Judge."

Bill stepped from behind his large mahogany partner desk as the ladies entered his office. "So good to see you again ladies and under such different, more pleasant circumstances. And, this lovely lady must be your grandmother, Rosa Lee."

"That's correct," Granny replied as she reached to shake hands with the attorney.

"Ida Mae gave me the details of your dilemma on the telephone late last evening," Wallace continued. "I must say the timing for what you have in mind could not have been better. I will be defending some clients in Judge Sidney Duff's court next week. One is a well-publicized case and I'm sure the courtroom will be crowded. I'm also sure that the case will take at least two days. It should be rather easy for you to conceal yourself among the spectators if you sit in the back of the room, wearing the disguise I've been made aware of.

"May I suggest neither of your granddaughters accompany you since they have been in his courtroom before? Believe me, this judge forgets very little. And I must ask that His Honor never know I am aware of your scheme. I may have other cases to be tried before him, you understand."

"I beg to differ Mr. Wallace. He forgot he asked me to marry him nearly half century ago. Will one of you girls bring me back to Mt. Airy next Sunday so I can get a room?" she asked.

"Nonsense," the attorney interjected. "You are welcome to stay with the wife and me. After all, that's the least we can do in light of all the help you folks provided our family during the time of our misfortune."

"You're alright for a city feller," Rosa Lee said.

"I can see we are going to have an exciting time during your stay." Wallace commented. He scribbled something on the back of one of his business cards and handed it to Mary Sue. "When you ladies come back to town next Sunday, please drop Rosa Lee off at this address. My wife and I will be expecting her."

All three ladies spent the remainder of the day browsing through the stores on Main Street. While still in Mt. Airy, Rosa Lee had been told so many good things about the Wallace family that she felt they were no longer strangers. Any apprehension about spending time with them faded. In fact, she was looking forward to getting to know them better.

Rosa Lee's plans were beginning to take shape. Things were working out much better than she could have imagined, so she decided to push her luck a little further. "Hey, girls, it's Friday."

she began, "Since it's nearing suppertime, why don't we drive up to Mama's Home Cooking for chicken and dumplings? It's not that far, and it will be my treat of course."

"Why not?" Ida Mae agreed. "Randolph might have a good-looking unmarried relative who also likes chicken and dumplings and drives a Cadillac. Mary Sue is still looking you know."

"Maybe so, let's go find out." Granny chuckled.

It was almost sundown when they arrived at the diner, and a day much different from when they were there earlier. There was no evidence of the down-pouring rain that had fallen a few days before or the dense fog that normally covered the mountaintop. It was a rather warm evening for early December with not a cloud in the sky.

"You're in luck, Granny," Mary Sue teased as Ida Mae pulled up along side Randolph's robin-egg blue Caddy. The freshly polished paint mirrored the neon lights of the sign over the restaurant door.

"If Mr. Patrick does have a son like Sis described, I hope his Cadillac is green," Mary Sue continued her teasing as they walked inside.

There were not many patrons, so it was not difficult to locate the person of interest. He was seated in the exact same booth where he had been when they first met. A half-filled cup of coffee sat in front of him, and he was reading the evening paper. One would guess he was waiting to be served. He was so intent on what he was reading, he didn't even notice when the ladies seated themselves at the bar. Granny made sure to take the seat nearest his booth, of course.

Irene placed a menu in front of each of them and welcomed them back.

"At least it's not raining this time so we won't have to spend the night," Granny stated in a voice louder than normal. Her comment fell on deaf ears but she did not give up. She cleared her throat so many times the girls were afraid the other customers might think she had something contagious.

In a little while Irene came back to the bar, bringing a tall glass of water for each of them. "Are you girls ready to order?" she asked.

Before either of them could respond, Randolph looked up from his newspaper. "Hi there, ladies. How are the three of you this evening?"

"Why, hello. Is that you Randy?" Granny answered.

Mary Sue had just taken a large gulp from her glass and Granny's reply brought on such an outburst of laughter she sent a spray of water completely across the bar, most of it landing on Irene. "Ex-ex-excuse me," she stammered as she covered her face and headed for the door. A full ten minutes passed before she had composed herself enough to return. When she did, Granny was in the booth with Randolph and Ida Mae was still at the bar overseeing two plates of Mama's famous chicken and dumplings.

"Must be nice to be graceful," Ida Mae began ribbing.

"I wouldn't know about being graceful, but it sure is nice to be entertained, especially the way Granny does it."

The sister's finished their meal much earlier than the other couple and pretended to be enjoying the music on the jukebox, allowing them more time to visit. When finally it was time to leave, they overheard Randolph ask, "Will I see you in two weeks?"

"We'll see," Granny replied in a tone that would lead one to think she was unsure.

"She must have made an impression," Mary Sue whispered.

"Right, but I think she looks tired, too much excitement for a lady her age, you think?"

When they had driven a few miles, Mary Sue turned to look at Rosa Lee who was riding in the back seat. She could see by the passing car lights that her back was toward the side window, arms folded, legs outstretched, and she was smiling like the cat that had just eaten the canary.

"Well Granny, what do you think of Mr. Patrick now that you've gotten to know him better?"

The only response was the sound of gentle snoring.

Chapter Three

THE DISGUISE

The weekend in Winston was hectic. Rosa Lee acted like a teenage girl who was preparing for her first date. One moment she seemed excited at the possibility of seeing Sidney again; the next, she expressed resentment toward him for leaving her.

Sometimes she would talk about her new friend Randolph and all the things she had learned about him; other times she acted as if nothing she'd learned about him mattered. Her behavior sure had the girls bewildered, but they had definitely decided Granny was tired of being a widow. She was surely out to find her a man. She even found it humorous when the ladies kidded her about which of her fellers might be their next grandpa.

She had planned her trip back to Mt. Airy down to the last detail. When Sunday morning rolled around, she was packed and ready to go. Although she was still a little apprehensive about spending time with the lawyer and his wife, she was willing to withstand that minor inconvenience in order to spend time in the courtroom. She was determined to learn all she could about this fellow she once thought she knew so well before she made her presence known.

Learning that Sidney had become successful was no surprise to her. His ambitious nature, intelligence, and eagerness to succeed dictated that would be the case. But, she was not going to leave Mt. Airy without learning how a former moonshine runner could have become a circuit court judge.

It was the middle of the afternoon when Ida Mae pulled into the driveway at the address Bill had given her. The attorney was pushing golf balls across a freshly manicured lawn toward a large tin can that lay on its side several feet away. Mrs. Wallace was reclining on the patio sipping a frosted glass of lemonade. She was trying to coach her husband by telling him how far he missed his target after each stroke.

"Sorry, if we're early," Ida Mae apologized. "Mary Sue is performing at one of the nightspots this evening, and we need to get back to Winston."

"Not at all," Bill greeted them. "We're glad you've arrived before suppertime. This beautiful lady is Betty Ann, my wife; and I've made reservations for the three of us at The Wild Steer."

"That's a steak house down town," Betty Ann explained. "Care for some lemonade ladies?"

"Thanks, but no, we must be going. Have Bill give us a call when you want us to come back for you, Granny," Ida Mae instructed.

Rosa Lee graciously accepted the lemonade as she watched her granddaughters make their departure. She sat next to Betty Ann and watched as ball after ball rolled past the tin cup.

"Is that golf you're playing, Mr. Wallace?" She asked.

"Just Bill, please. And yes, but I'm just practicing; and as you can see, I really need to."

"Looks like fun, mind if I try?"

"Not at all; it would be nice to have some competition. Betty Ann doesn't care much for the game." Bill chose another club from his highly polished golf bag and presented it to Rosa Lee. He painstakingly instructed her on the proper stance and the correct way to hold the putter. After about fifteen minutes of what seemed like professional instructions, he asked. "Got it Rosa Lee?"

"I think so."

Bill gathered several balls that were scattered around the tin can and lined them up in a straight row. "We'll take three shots each; just watch and you'll see how it's done." He stroked the first three balls in the row and watched as they slowly rolled past the can. "Your turn," he said.

Granny planted her feet, raised her club, and gave the next ball in line a brisk stroke. It hit the inside of the can with a loud ping. Her next two strokes proved to be as accurate as the first. Both times the ball found its target. Bill turned his blushing face toward Betty Ann, "Isn't it about time to get dressed to go eat?"

"Not until you finish teaching Rosa Lee how to play golf," she teased.

"Beginners luck," Rosa Lee insisted.

"With luck like, that I need you at the defense table with me tomorrow."

The remainder of the afternoon was spent getting better-acquainted and exchanging stories about The Honorable Sidney Duff. Rosa Lee told how she and the judge had grown up in the same community. She also told they had been high school sweethearts and had planned to marry but gave no hint about why the ceremony never took place.

The young attorney told Rosa Lee he had only known the judge a few years and had limited knowledge of his background. As far as anyone knew he obtained his law degree at some college in West Virginia where he had practiced for some time before moving to North Carolina. Some said he had married late in life, that a fatal heart attack claimed his missus a few years later; and from that time, he has remained pretty much a loner.

Bill could speak to his credibility as a member of the judiciary, however. The judge was viewed as fair and impartial and most always lenient to first-time non-violent offenders. He believed everyone was entitled to one mistake and deserved a second chance. But, he could also be as harsh when necessary. One thing Wallace knew for certain was that the judge's record keeping capability was second to none. He kept transcript copies of every case that ever came before him. Only members of the bar association and his closest friends knew that these copies were locked away somewhere on his two-acre estate a few miles outside of town.

The attorney felt he had told their guest very little about her friend of years ago. But, Rosa Lee, on the other hand, was intrigued by what she had heard. And, she was even more determined to learn what had taken place in his life since she last saw him.

Betty Ann, whose sense of humor equally matched her good looks, sat quietly by listening to Rosa Lee and her husband exchange stories about the judge. Although she had never met the gentleman, their conversation aroused her curiosity. So much so, she was becoming anxious to know what Rosa Lee hoped might take place as the next chapter of their lives unfolded. But, as the evening approached, she found it necessary to interrupt.

"We had better get dressed for dinner, Honey, unless you would rather stay home and give our guest another golfing lesson." An hour later, they were being ushered to their table at The Wild Steer.

Rosa Lee felt somewhat out of place; she had never been in such a fine restaurant. The only lighting was candles located in carefully selected places throughout the establishment. Maroon-colored linens covered every table. Brass rings encircled matching cloth napkins and more silverware than most mountain folks owned lay on either side of each plate. The aroma of food being prepared in the kitchen was enough to whet one's appetite even if they were not hungry.

Most of the patrons were casually dressed for a Sunday evening, but the jewelry they wore made it evident they were not from the poor side of town.

Rosa Lee was careful not to do anything that might embarrass herself and was relieved when the attorney suggested what they might have for their evening meal. He ordered for each of them, and they sipped wine while waiting to be served. Granny drank from her glass sparingly but decided that if the moonshiners back home had tried to sell this stuff they would have been run out of the county. In her opinion, she thought it tasted like rotten grape juice.

Rosa Lee excused herself to go to the ladies room and was barely on her feet when Bill hurriedly took her by the hand. "Not yet," he said.

Surprised, she stood motionless as she waited for an explanation.

"There he is," he said in a voice barely above a whisper.

"Who?" Betty Ann wanted to know, bewildered at what had just taken place.

"The judge."

"Not Judge Duff," she said.

"The one and only."

Rosa Lee sank back in her chair. She sat speechless as she watched the waiter escort Sidney to his table. She breathed a sigh of relief when he began reading from the menu and appeared to be uninterested in his surroundings. Tiny shadows created by the glimmer of a nearby candle danced gingerly on his silver gray hair. He looked tired and somewhat older than she would have imagined but still as handsome as she remembered. It was hard for her to understand how someone with his appearance and social standing had never remarried.

She hardly touched her food and seldom took her eyes from across the dining room. At times he looked so lonely she fought the temptation to go be with him. But then, she needed to learn more before deciding if she wanted to renew an old friendship. After all, more than half century had passed since he'd promised to purchase his Model-T and come back for her. So what difference could a few more days make? They waited until the judge had made his exit before they left the restaurant.

Chapter Four

THE COURTROOM

Monday morning found the courtroom crowded so Rosa Lee had no trouble getting lost among the spectators. She barely found room in one of the backseats before the bailiff asked everyone to rise. A tingle, like an electrical current, shot through her body as he announced court was in session and would be presided over by The Honorable Judge Sidney Duff. She was filled with sheer disbelief that, after so many years, some of the feelings for her old flame still lingered. She was unsure whether she wanted to pursue a renewed relationship; she would make that decision later. Right now she just wanted to see the judge at work.

Rosa Lee sat, completely unnoticed, through two days of court proceedings listening to one civil case after another. Most of the cases only required the settlement of a small debt or a dispute between neighbors. These were cases of little importance, except to those directly involved; but she found them informative and sometimes rather entertaining. She was fascinated by the attorneys ability to defend their clients, especially her new friend Bill Wallace. And, she was impressed with the judge's fairness in rendering his decisions; but she felt he probably did as most other judges would have done in similar situations.

It was during the third day of court that Rosa Lee was to learn the true character of the Honorable Judge Duff. It was the case that had the community in an uproar and filled the courtroom to capacity. The case involved a young man accused of breaking into a grocery store owned by John Snider, one of the wealthiest and most disliked men in the city.

Snider was not only the proprietor of the grocery store, he owned or had interest in other businesses in town, all of which he'd inherited. He was a member of almost every social club and had somehow weaseled himself into being elected president of the City Council. And, because of his standing in the city, he made sure the local paper made the most of the case. He'd more than once bragged to the media that no one would rip him off without being punished to the full extent of the law. It made absolutely no difference that the fellow accused had been unemployed for several weeks and had taken only food for his family. He'd show this generation of young hoodlums. After all, the prosecuting attorney was one his Saturday morning golfing buddies.

After rendering the customary instructions to the spectators the bailiff stated the next case before the court. "John Snider vs. Johnny Evans."

"Are the attorneys for both sides ready to proceed?" the judge wanted to know.

The state's attorney, who was seated beside Mr. Snider at a table directly in front of the jury box, rose to his feet. "Well, oh, I suppose so," he snarled.

"Is there some difficulty?" the judge asked.

"It's just that I was told Judge Baker would be hearing this case."

"I really hate to disappoint you, Mr. Prosecutor, but because you and Arnold, I mean Judge Baker, are sometimes golfing partners at the country club, he chose to excuse himself. I do hope you have no objections."

"I guess not; let's get this show on the road," the prosecutor snapped as he gazed back over the courtroom, hoping to make an impression on Mr. Snider and the spectators. However, he immediately learned that the impression he'd made on the judge was not a favorable one.

"I beg your pardon, Sir," the judge scolded. "Are we just a little over confident this morning?"

"Not at all Your Honor; we're just anxious to see this crook get what he deserves. Maybe some time behind bars will make him think twice before he pulls a caper like this again."

"That will be for the court to decide, Sir. Is the defense ready?"

"We are, Sir," defense attorney Wallace replied.

"Then since you are in such a hurry to get started, call your first witness, Mr. Prosecutor."

Attorney Wallace stood facing the bench, "If it please the court, that won't be necessary, my client pleads guilty with extenuating circumstances which we wish to explain."

"Then please continue, if the prosecutor has no objections."

"Not at all, I can hardly wait to hear what worthless excuse the defendant has for committing such an offense."

Mr. Wallace told the court that Mr. Evans had been without a job for months. He explained he had a wife and two small children to support and that his unemployment checks ended some weeks ago. He also explained that his client had tried unsuccessfully to find work at every business in the city, Mr. Snider's not excluded. The attorney also made the court aware of the fact that his client sold his only automobile, at less that it's true value, in order to purchase food for his family. He stressed the fact that his client had never before been in trouble, and food was the only items taken at the time the crime was committed. In conclusion Attorney Wallace informed the court that Mr. Evans had been incarcerated for more than a month because he was unable to make bail. "Therefore, Your Honor, my client pleads guilty and asks for mercy."

"Does the prosecution have any comments?"

The prosecutor exchanged words with Mr. Snider, in a tone not auditable to anyone else. "We certainly do, Your Honor. Being unemployed, regardless of the size of his family, should by no means give the defendant the right to unlawfully enter a business establishment and take food or anything else for that matter. Therefore, we demand he be punished to the full extent of the law."

"Speaking of food, I'm hungry gentlemen. Court is in recess until two o'clock; I'll let you know my decision at that time."

Everyone stood as the judge made his exit before they left the courtroom. Rosa Lee watched as a uniformed officer escorted the defendant out of the building. She fought the urge to go find the judge and do her best to convince him to go easy on the young man. For more reasons than she wanted to think about at the time, that thought was out of the question.

"Lunch as usual?" Bill questioned.

Rosa Lee and the young attorney made their way out of the building, crossed the street to a small diner and ordered the special of the day. "Will Sid, I mean Judge Duff, send the young man back to jail?" Rosa Lee asked just as the waitress sat a large bowl of vegetable soup in front of each of them.

"Can't say. I've had very few cases heard by Judge Duff. He is retired and only substitutes, you know. However, he has always treated my clients fairly and has been lenient when circumstances would allow. But, you must remember the plaintiff is a, pardon my expression, big shot in the city and will expect the judge to hand down a harsh sentence. It is well known the judge maintains complete control while on the bench and will not permit anyone's being disrespectful to the witnesses or to the court. I suppose you were aware that my worthy opponent had almost pushed the judge's patience to the limit."

Rosa Lee had hurriedly finished her lunch and was anxious to get back to the courthouse. "No doubt," she replied. "Let's go see if his attitude has anything to do with the sentencing."

By the time Rosa Lee re-entered the courtroom, it was almost filled to capacity. The only seat available was on the aisle near the center of the room. She squeezed herself into the vacant space and tried to conceal herself behind an oversized gentleman seated in front of her.

The accused was occupying a seat at the defense table: and from where she sat, Rosa Lee could tell he was so nervous his hands were trembling. A good-looking young lady sat directly behind him trying unsuccessfully to prevent the occasional tear from falling.

"All rise," the bailiff bellowed; "court is back in session."

As the judge entered the room, the prosecutor gave Mr. Snider a pat on his shoulder, an indication that they were about to hear a sentence to their liking.

"Will the defendant please stand?" The statement sounded more like a request than a command. "Do you have anything to say before I make my ruling?"

"No, Sir, Your Honor."

"Then I will tell you, that while at lunch, I had my secretary make some phone calls to various business owners in town. Oddly enough, every one of them remembered your applying for, almost begging, for employment. Regretfully none of them had an opening for you, which solidifies what you have told the court. I must say that although I cannot condone the action you chose, I'm not sure I would have done differently. Therefore I am sentencing you to time served; and as many hours labor in the plaintiff's employ as is necessary to pay for the merchandise that was taken."

A sigh of relief filled the courtroom as the young lady burst into tears and threw her arms around her husband. Rosa Lee was sure Sidney was staring straight at her as he ordered the spectators to calm down.

Snider sprang to his feet, "You have got to be kidding," he growled, "That's nothing more than a slap on the wrist. Why! He should be locked up!"

"I am not in the habit of kidding, Sir; and if I hear one more outcry, I will see that you're locked up the equal number of hours for being in contempt." He watched, as the prosecutor almost demanded Snider sit down.

The judge gave Rosa Lee a questioning look as he slowly made way toward his chambers. She was so filled with admiration for her old beau she would have liked to give him a firm embrace, but she was careful not to move until the door closed behind him.

Wallace had no more work for the day, and the afternoon was still young. An unusually warm November breeze greeted the couple as they stepped onto the street in front of the courthouse. Not a cloud could be seen in the clear blue autumn sky, and neither had further plans for the day.

"Want to go back inside and say hello to the judge?" Bill asked.

Rosa Lee toyed with the idea for a moment before deciding she would wait until later. "Why don't we go home and practice our golf game," she teased. "I'll see if the girls will come get me tonight, and maybe they'll take me back to Virginia this weekend. I'm kind of homesick, and I'd like to stop at that little diner up on the mountain. They serve some fabulous chicken and dumplings. You should try them sometime."

Rosa Lee had no trouble talking the two young ladies into taking her back to the mountains. In fact, they were so anxious to see how their parents liked living in a different home, they wanted they leave early the next morning. But, when Granny suggested they wait until late afternoon, they knew exactly what she had in mind.

Ida Mae winked at Mary Sue. "Okay with me; we'll run down to Ike's place and have a delicious seafood dinner before we leave."

"Oh, that's not necessary, we'll just grab a bite on the way home," Granny replied.

"Wouldn't have a burning desire for another plate of chicken and dumplings, would you?" Mary Sue teased.

"Could be, and they always taste better when they're shared with someone of the opposite sex."

The girls did as their grandmother wished. They pulled in front of the diner just about sundown. There were several cars in the parking lot but the blue Cadillac she hoped to see was not there. They went inside and took seats at the bar. The waitress, who had come to know them quite well, asked if they were having their Friday special.

"Not yet," Rosa Lee was quick to reply, "just coffee, we're waiting for someone."

"Oh, if you mean Randy, he came in earlier; but he's already gone. Acted as if he was in somewhat of a hurry. There was a well-dressed gentleman came in looking for him not ten minutes after he left."

"Then bring each of us a hamburger," she sighed.

"Lost your taste for the dumplings?" Ida Mae asked.

"Yep, let's hurry and eat; maybe we can get home before everyone's in bed."

They finished eating, got into the car and were about ready to pull away when Rosa Lee suddenly decided she needed to use the bathroom. Once inside, she scribbled her address and phone number on a napkin and asked Irene if she would please see that her friend got the information. "You know whom," she added.

The waitress winked as she tucked the message into the pocket of her apron.

Rosa Lee left the restaurant disappointed, dejected and bewildered. She had never felt so uncertain about her future at any time in her sixty-plus years. The judge, she had to admit, stirred emotions she thought had vanished decades earlier. He had accomplished much in life; and she, on the other hand, was the same country bumpkin he'd abandoned when they were teenagers. She had every intention of renewing some sort of relationship but after seeing and learning more about him, she became fearful she would not be able to fit into his lifestyle.

She was also beginning to question why she had become so interested in the stranger she met at Mama's Home Cooking. After all, he might be more into the elite style of living than the judge. Right now, it didn't really matter; she might not ever see him again.

What did matter to her most was she was becoming restless. She had been content living with her son and his family since the death of his father; in fact, she felt her presence was almost necessary. To keep the huge farm and the big house running smoothly required the labor of many hands. There was always something that needed to be done, and she was more than willing to do her share. The place they now lived was barely large enough for Ira, Mary Ellen and the twins, so she felt the urge to move. She didn't think of herself as being old; she was still reasonably attractive, and the thought of marrying again was becoming more interesting.

She'd give this matter some thought later. It had been a long day, and she was tired; she might even give up on all men and just move in with Gertie.

CHAPTER FIVE

BACK TO THE MOUNTAIN

Ida Mae pulled into the driveway of the family's new dwelling shortly before midnight, but it certainly didn't feel like home. The small house looked so tiny in comparison to the huge rambling farmhouse that had been their home for most of her life.

She did not follow Granny and her younger sister into the house. Instead, she sat on the top porch step and gazed at the outline of their former home, clearly illuminated by a golden harvest moon.

She let her mind wander back to the many warm summer evenings she and members of the family had sat on the porch of that home sharing each other's hopes, dreams, and sometimes troubles and disappointments.

The memory of her little sister's harmonizing with one of the country music singers on the radio seemed as if it were happening at that very moment.

Memories of the bitter cold winter nights when the entire family was still at home, were as vivid as if she were reading from the pages of yesterday's diary. She could almost see her older brother John Robert hopelessly trying to beat her dad at a game of checkers, her little twin brothers busily constructing a new slingshot, or her mother and Granny busily sewing together the pieces of their next prize-winning quilt. She could almost hear the crackling of the logs burning in the fireplace and feel their warmth as the shadows of the flames danced across the ceiling. She was so engrossed in her daydreaming that the sound of her father's police car pulling into the driveway startled her.

"Well, isn't this a pleasant surprise? What brings you back home so soon? And, why are you sitting out here in the cold this time of night?"

"One question at a time, please, Daddy. It's good to know you're happy to see me; Granny got homesick, and I guess I just haven't noticed there is a chill in the air."

"Was Mom happy to be reunited with her old boyfriend?"

"She hasn't met him yet; I'll tell you all about it tomorrow," she said as they made their way inside.

"That's good; I'm not convinced she was as anxious to find him as she would like us to think. As soon as I bought this place, she began talking about getting out on her own. I realize it's not as large as we need, but it was the best I could do on such short notice. We all know Baxter leased the farm to the Sutter family as a way of getting revenge, and rumors have it he's not finished yet."

"Who are the Sutters, and where do they come from?" she asked.

"I have no idea—somewhere in the northern section of the county. Seem to be a friendly sort, a little backwards maybe; but they wave or speak every time they pass. I'm told there's only old man Sutter, his wife, and two overgrown boys who are in their late twenties. I've also heard they know much more about raising Cain than they do about raising corn, hay or cattle.

"Anyway, Mom feels there is simply not enough space for all of us, and she should move. She's aware there's no way she could survive on her meager income. I'm afraid she will do something she'll be sorry for later."

"You don't mean getting married! Granny?"

"Can't ever tell; you know your grandmother. She can be as stubborn as a mule and as hard-headed as a goat; guess that comes from living on the farm so long."

"You don't think Baxter would be so foolish as to do something to harm one of you, do you Daddy?"

"Could be, but we'll discuss this tomorrow. You look tired."

The four-room dwelling was small, so small, Ida Mae felt claustrophobic. Her mother and sister were sitting at a table in the kitchen that also served as a dining room. The master bedroom, if one could call it that, was for her parents and the only other bedroom she would share with Mary Sue. The twins, Kevin and Kervin were bedded down on a pallet in one corner of the living room, and Granny was already asleep on the sofa.

"I know you girls and your daddy must be worn out so let's all turn in," Mary Ellen suggested. "We're a little cramped," she added, her voice was almost apologetic, "but we'll have to make do until we can make other arrangements."

Ida Mae slipped into bed beside her sister. She stretched her tired body between the cool cotton sheets and stared out the window at the moonlit sky. "This will never do," she whispered. "I understand why Granny has suddenly become so restless. If we don't get our folks out of this little cracker box, they'll all go crazy."

"As soon as I record my first hit record . . . good night, Sis."

Her sister was asleep in minutes, but Ida Mae lay awake for hours. She knew her family could never be happy living in such close quarters. They had grown accustomed to living in a large two-story farmhouse with enough room to do whatever they pleased. There was no way they would adjust to this type of life; living in sight of their previous home didn't make it any easier. Maybe someday Mary Sue would have a hit record. After all she was performing in some of the most well-known nightclubs in Winston. However, for now she felt she and Jake must do something. She decided she would talk it over with him as soon as she got back home. She was afraid if they didn't do something right away, Granny might be bringing a new member into the family. Not that her grandmother wasn't looking out for her own welfare; her old beau, a semi-retired judge, must have accumulated a small fortune and her most recent male acquaintance drove around in a new Cadillac.

She was awakened the following morning by the aroma of fresh-brewed coffee and the sound of her twin brothers romping in the yard just outside her bedroom window.

These surroundings snapped her back to her concerns of the evening before.

The rumors her daddy mentioned about Baxter's intentions of being more vengeful really concerned her. Being ousted as sheriff was enough embarrassment to cause him to move out of the county. To have her father, whom he had fired as chief deputy, take his job might have been enough to push him over the edge. If that were true, she knew Baxter well enough to know he would stop at nothing to bring harm to her family. She was sure her mother was being shielded from the rumors, but she intended to learn all she could before leaving.

"If you're planning to have breakfast in bed, Ida Mae, forget it," Kevin yelled.

"Be right there, but don't wait for me."

"We're not. Kervin is already eating his sixth biscuit," he teased.

Ida Mae slipped into her robe and joined the other members of her family. She missed the times when her family had gathered at their table discussing the events of a new day, not to mention the wonderful meal they had shared. This had been one of those days, and she hated having to leave, but Mary Sue was scheduled to sing at one of Winston's most elite nightspots at eight that evening.

She followed Ira outside and was about to inquire about the rumors just as his police radio sounded off. "Sheriff, if you copy, there's two or three drunks having a fight down town on main street," one of his deputies reported. "I'll take care of it but just wanted you to know. ETA fifteen minutes."

"Ten-four. Don't those fools know it's Saturday, and they're not supposed to start fighting until after dark. I'll be there by the time you are."

"Not without me," Ida Mae said as she jumped into the seat beside her daddy. "I haven't seen a good fight since I was in high school."

She was not at all interested in who was fighting, but she knew this was a chance to get him alone and learn what she could about those rumors. They arrived in town ahead of the deputy and drove the entire length of both streets in their small town, but everything seemed as peaceful as Sunday morning at church time.

"Oh, no! Not again!" Ira swore under his breath as he shifted the squad car into second gear. The rear tires of the Dodge smoked when he rammed the accelerator to the floor. He keyed the mike on his radio and gave Deputy Barton instructions to turn and go to his house at once and stay until he got there.

Ida Mae's heart skipped a beat. She grabbed her daddy's arm, and in a voice that was almost pleading, asked, "What is going on?"

"Baxter! He never lets up. Whenever a call comes in I never know if it's legit or if he or one of his cronies is sending us on a wild goose chase so he can harm us in someway. That's why I was so late getting in last night. I'd heard he was back in the county and I was trying to hunt him down. I can never catch sight of him, but he seems to always know where I am. You didn't know it, but one of my deputies had our house under surveillance until I got home. I didn't take the rumors serious until I left for work about daylight one morning and discovered a small dead animal lying on our front porch."

"Maybe a dog put it there," Ida Mae suggested.

"Not with a threatening note attached to it's body. There have been other such messages left on my car and slipped under my office door when I was out. Promise you won't mention any of this to your mother. It would only cause her to worry."

"What can be done to stop him?" His daughter's voice was trembling.

"Nothing until we catch him red-handed. Threatening an officer of the law is a serious crime, but I don't know if it's me he really wants to harm."

Ida Mae fell silent for a moment, her mind racing through the events of the last few months. It was her mother and Granny who really brought about Baxter's downfall. If Granny hadn't secretly recorded the Sheriff's conversation when he stooped so low as to use blackmail in order to get her mother to go out with him, he would still be in office. This brought on a new meaning of the word fear.

"What could he hope to gain?" she asked. "He has been disgraced, lost his position as sheriff, and shamed to the point of having to move out of the county."

Chapter Six

GRANNY HAS A DATE

Winter passed slowly for the Duncan family. The first big snowfall came the middle of December and was followed by another and then another. It seemed the whole world was blanketed in white and would never be green again. Wind-driven snow covered the northern sides of everything visible above the ever-deepening drifts. Any attempt to clear the mounds from the gravel road that ran in front of their home had ceased, so traffic was at a standstill.

Christmas season came and went without any of the usual celebrating. This was the first year all their family had not been together for the holiday. John Robert and his bride-to-be were busy making plans for their upcoming wedding. Jake and Ida Mae were running over with houseguests who had a family member hospitalized, and Mary Sue was busy studying for mid-term exams. Ira's time was devoted to assisting those having difficulty battling the harsh weather, so he was seldom at home. That left Mary Ellen, Rosa Lee and the twins seemingly imprisoned in their tiny dwelling.

Each time the girls called they encouraged their grandmother to come spend time in the Carolinas. As each night grew colder and the snow got deeper, the thought of doing just that became more appealing. After all, she hadn't given up on the idea of becoming reacquainted with Sidney. She had been a good wife, had even grown to truly admire the man she'd married and had fathered her only child, but she still harbored memories of her first real love. So as winter began giving way to the infancy of spring, she decided the Carolinas were where she wanted to be. Then when Ida Mae announced she was coming home for a few days, Rosa Lee began packing her bags.

It was no accident Ida Mae started back to Winston on Friday afternoon. She sensed Rose Lee's need for a change of scenery and hoped a good portion of chicken and dumplings might be just what she needed. If by chance Randolph was there, her grandmother's depression brought about because of the harsh winter might suddenly dissipate. Her diagnosis had been correct, and the cure was even more astonishing! The minute Ida Mae pulled into the restaurant near the top of the mountain, the old familiar gleam reappeared in Rosa Lee's eyes. Ida Mae parked beside the blue caddie and watched as Rosa Lee used the side-view mirror to make herself look her best.

When they entered the restaurant it seemed Randolph had been expecting them. He smiled at the duo and beckoned them to join him. As if on cue, Irene sat a large plate of the day's special in front of him. "Two more," he told the waitress as he looked to the ladies for their approval.

As the threesome finished their dinner, Randolph asked if Rosa Lee would like to go for a drive. Before she could answer, he immediately promised to have her home in Winston no later than midnight. Rosa Lee blushed and, like a young lady asking permission to go on her first date, turned to her granddaughter. Ida Mae hesitated a moment before nodding her approval. "Be sure you have her home by midnight," she warned.

Ida Mae left the restaurant with a feeling of apprehension. She drove to Winston feeling guilty for allowing Rosa Lee to go riding with someone she hardly knew and maybe to some place she's never heard of. One word would have prevented Rosa Lee from accepting Randolph's invitation. But, who was she to tell her grandmother what to do? By the time she turned onto Chestnut Street, it was almost dark, and she was on the edge of panic. What if she had made the wrong decision? There was nothing she could do now but wait. That was exactly what she was going to do. She greeted Jake with a smile and a kiss, participated in a bit of small talk with their guests, who were fewer than when she had left, and waited for everyone to go to bed. She made herself a steaming hot cup of tea, sat on the front porch and gazed at the stars through the budding limbs of the magnolia trees, waiting for Granny to come home.

When the large Grandfather clock in the hallway struck once, she knew she only had half-hour to wait. But, at quarter past midnight she began pacing the floor. The echoing sounds of the city were becoming less audible, and her heartbeat was becoming louder and faster. She'd wait only fifteen minutes more, she decided; and then she'd wake Jake. She was about to do just that; but as she reached the front entrance, she could see the bright beams of headlights turning onto Chestnut Street. She barely had time to conceal herself behind a high-backed rocking chair when Randolph's Cadillac came to a stop in front of their home.

Randy escorted Rosa Lee to the edge of the porch, thanked her for a wonderful evening, strolled back to the caddie and drove away. Rosa Lee stood for a moment as if reliving the events of the evening, then mumbled as she made her way inside, "I'm sure glad everyone's already in bed."

Ida Mae breathed a sigh of relief and whispered, "If she only knew," as the large front door slowly closed.

The next morning Granny was up at the crack of dawn. The sound of pots and pans rattling in the kitchen was enough to wake everyone in the house.

Jake sat up in bed and began shaking Ida Mae. "Wake up! Sounds like someone's taking the place apart."

Ida Mae, being a sound sleeper, had heard nothing; but she had a good idea what was happening. As the banging sounds continued, she knew she was right. "Oh, it's only Granny" she yawned. "She's always been an early riser; go back to sleep."

"Granny! You mean Rosa Lee? How did she get here?"

"Her date brought her home around midnight."

Jake removed the pillow Ida Mae had just placed over her head and began shaking her again. "Wake up, dear, somebody's destroying the downstairs; and you're having a bad dream."

"It's just Granny. Go down and help her with breakfast and call me when it's ready. I'll explain everything in the morning."

"Morning," he groaned. "It is morning, but just barely," he said as he looked at the clock and saw it was almost six a.m. He knew Ida Mae hadn't heard a word, so he slipped on his robe and headed downstairs. As he entered the kitchen, he was greeted by Rosa Lee's smiling face.

"Hope you're hungry," she chirped. "I should have had breakfast ready, but I got in a little late last night."

Suddenly, he realized Ida Mae had not been having a bad dream. It was he who was having a nightmare! "No one gets up this early on a Saturday morning," he said under his breath as he headed back upstairs to demand an explanation. He snuggled between the warm covers and immediately decided to enjoy another couple hour's sleep. He could hear about this new romance later. Twenty minutes later his thought of having a nightmare became a reality when Rosa Lee yelled from the foot of the stairs, "Come and get it." Jake and Ida Mae sat up in bed, startled by the unusual noise at such an early hour. Jake gave Ida Mae a disgruntled look and asked if she wanted to go down and send Granny back to bed or if he should do it.

"She's just excited," Ida Mae insisted." You know how it is on your first date."

"With all the goings on, I can barely remember our last date," he said mockingly. As he headed to the bathroom, he opened the bedroom door and was about to yell downstairs just as Ida Mae interrupted.

"Jake! Don't you dare! Let her enjoy the moment."

By this time Jake was wide-awake, "Okay," he joked, "but next time tell her to spend the night."

In a few minutes, they were seated at the breakfast table with Rosa Lee and their hospitality guests, overlooking a meal that was surely worth getting out of bed early to enjoy.

Chapter Seven

THE FIRST DRIVING LESSON

Rosa Lee shuffled around the house for the next few days like a teenager experiencing her first high school crush. It was not until midweek she told Ida Mae why she was so jolly. "Randy," as Granny now called him, was picking her up at ten o'clock Friday morning; and they were going to spend the day together.

As promised, Randolph arrived right on time. Rosa Lee met him at the door looking more radiant than Ida Mae had seen her in years. "See you tonight," she told her granddaughter who was standing on the lawn enjoying the warm morning sunshine.

"Have a good day, and sleep late in the morning," Ida Mae whispered.

As the couple approached the Cadillac, Randolph handed Rosa Lee the keys.

"Care to drive?" he asked.

"Oh, no, I've never driven an expensive automobile such as this; but maybe some other time." She turned toward her grand-daughter and smiled.

Just wait until I tell Jake about this little episode, Ida Mae thought as she rushed back inside for fear she would laugh out loud.

Rosa Lee spent the entire day with her friend Randolph and at least two or three days a week for the next month. She called home at regular intervals but made no mention of when she might go back to the mountains.

Ida Mae had not seen her grandmother so happy in years. Each day she was not with Randolph she had some new adventure to share, and Ida Mae was always anxious to lend an ear. She learned how the two of them had toured every scenic attraction in the western half of North Carolina, had eaten at some of the finest restaurants for miles around, and enjoyed an outdoor drama near Charlotte. "The trip to Charlotte was both business and pleasure," Rosa Lee was pleased to add. "Randy collected money for a new Caddy, all in cash too. Remember he told us he had an interest in an automobile dealership."

Ida Mae and Jake would sit on the porch each evening enjoying the warmth of early spring and listening to the sounds on Main Street two blocks away. It was on one these evenings they both got an unbelievable surprise. A shiny black Cadillac came to a stop in front of their front lawn, and Randolph's blue automobile followed close behind.

Randolph got out of the lead car, and Rosa Lee got out of the one that followed. He gave the keys to the black one to Rosa Lee, gave her a quick peck on the cheek, waved to the folks on the porch, got into the blue car and drove off.

Rosa Lee strolled up to the porch, smiled at Jake and Ida Mae, sat in the porch swing and didn't a say word. Ida Mae, like Jake, knew she was waiting for some comment about her new adventure, but Ida Mae was determined to wait until she was asked. Anxiety, however finally got the best of her. "Is that a gift?" Ida Mae asked.

"Oh, no, it's not mine."

"She meant for us," Jake said, straining hard to keep from laughing.

Rosa Lee knew he was ribbing her a bit, but she was delighted to allow him the opportunity to have a little fun.

"Randolph will be back in the morning, and we'll deliver that new caddy to Charlotte."

"But you don't have a license," Ida Mae insisted.

"I know and I'm going to get one as soon as I learn how to do that darn parental parking. According to Randy, half the drivers in the state don't have a license."

"You must mean parallel parking," Ida Mae corrected as she turned aside so Rosa Lee could not see she was shaking with laughter.

"I believe that is what they call it. Anyway it's when you park between two vehicles without taking any bumpers or fenders off."

Ida Mae let the conversation drop for the moment; but the next day, she began questioning her grandmother about the gentleman with whom she was spending so much time. She learned she didn't know exactly where the fellow lived, the location of the dealership he supposedly partially owned, and almost nothing else about him in spite of what he had told her when they first met. This lack of knowledge was of little concern to Rosa Lee, but Ida Mae was beginning to question his character.

When she asked her grandmother about her knowing so little about Randolph, Rosa Lee was quick to remind her that his knowledge of her was about equal. She did confide in her that Randolph's automobile business was doing quite well and that they were delivering a new Cadillac almost every week.

"You accompany him on every delivery?"

"Certainly, dear, why not?"

Ida Mae quickly realized Rosa Lee thought she was prying so she let the conversation drop.

Another week passed without any mention of their relationship, but the following Saturday morning Rosa Lee could not wait to get Ida Mae alone to share the events of the previous evening. Their delivery the day before had been to Mt. Airy, and Randolph had been so excited about the transaction, he was in the mood to celebrate. So as promised, he took her to one of the finest restaurants in town, which as fate would have it was the very same restaurant where she and the Wallace's had dined a few weeks earlier. Luckily they were seated at one of the most dimly lit tables in the establishment because moments later, a waitress had ushered Sidney and a lady to the same table where he had been seated before.

Rosa Lee said nothing about their presence but was delighted she was seated in a position where she could see their every move. "The lady," she confided, "appeared to be much younger than her Sidney; but he seemed to be totally engrossed in their conversation. I'm sure Randy thought I was really interested in everything he was discussing; but little did he know, I was looking over his shoulder at the couple seated some distance away. I must admit I ate very slowly for fear of having Sidney recognize me as we were leaving. I must also tell you the longer I watched him, the more the embers I thought had grown cold years ago began to flame deep inside once more. Of course, I didn't see the need to tell Randolph I had visited the restaurant before."

"I bet you didn't see the need to tell him your first love was seated right behind him either," Ida Mae teased.

"Well, no."

Ida Mae was delighted to learn someone other than Randolph had captured her grandmother's interest if only for a few moments. She was even more pleased that someone was Sidney. Granny hadn't mentioned him in days, and Ida Mae was beginning to wonder if she had given up on him altogether. She was also beginning to question the character of this big-time automobile dealer with whom Granny was spending so much time. It was odd, she reasoned, that the automobiles he sold, which were almost always Cadillacs, were personally delivered. He explained, when Rosa Lee asked, that it was his way of showing a bit more gratitude. Nonetheless, Ida Mae was not as gullible as her granny.

She was not about to let the opportunity to renew Rosa Lee's interest in Sidney to slip away. "Mary Sue and I have wanted the three of us to go back to Mt. Airy shopping. What do you think Granny?"

Rosa Lee saw right through her granddaughter's motives for going to Mt. Airy. "I suppose we should try to learn a little more about the judge. Right?"

Ida Mae was about to come up with a clever answer, but Rosa Lee interrupted. "I really think that would be a waste of time. He seemed to really admire the pretty young lady he was having dinner with last evening, and I'm quite sure any chance of my competing with her would be out of the question."

"Does that mean you've given up already? You and Randolph aren't getting a little serious, are you?"

"Oh, no. Well he isn't anyway, but he is really good to me. He always treats me like a lady, and he lets me drive his Caddy each time we make a delivery. I really enjoy spending time with him, and I'm always home by midnight," she quickly added.

Ida Mae knew Granny felt learning to drive was one of her greatest accomplishments.

"What about our shopping trip? We'll leave early and spend the day if you like."

"Wonderful, then I'd like to go home for a spell. When I talked to Ira, something tells me things are not going as well as he would have us believe."

Immediately Ida Mae started putting a plan together. She'd call Bill Wallace; have him invite Judge Duff out to dinner with the pretense of discussing some legal matter, and then secretly plan for the three of them to dine at the same restaurant. Mary Sue thought her sister's plan was a great idea, and she was sure they would have no difficulty convincing the attorney to play along. After all, their courthouse scheme had gone as planned.

The ladies were not accustomed to interfering with the private lives of another family member, but they were afraid their grandmother was becoming too involved with a fellow she knew too little about. After all, her initial interest in coming to North Carolina had been to get reacquainted with Sidney; and the girls intended to do whatever it took to make that happen.

So, in a couple of days, the three ladies were on their way to Mt. Airy. Mary Sue had made a list of the stores she wanted to shop in and Ida Mae had made plans to be alone for a while. One of their former house guests had moved to Mt. Airy, and she had been promising to visit at her first opportunity; at least that was what she told Granny. It was, of course, the only way she knew to find out all she could about Sidney.

It was Monday morning, and the streets weren't very crowded. Ida Mae dropped Mary Sue and her grandmother off at the first place on their shopping list and made a beeline to Bill Wallace's office. She'd made an appointment earlier; and as always, the attorney was happy to see her.

"Don't tell me you still haven't gotten those two old timers together," Bill teased as Ida Mae entered his office.

"Not yet, but we haven't given up."

"All right then, young lady, let's see what we can do to make this happen." He paged his receptionist and instructed her to phone the office of Judge Sidney Duff. "Tell them it's important I speak with him," he added.

A few moments later, the receptionist came on the desk intercom. "Sorry, sir, I was just informed the judge is on a fishing trip somewhere in the Ozarks and isn't due back for at least two weeks."

"Just our luck," Ida Mae sighed. "It appears as if we're never going to get those two back together. I've been told he's been seen in the company of a younger lady so he might not be as happy to see his old flame, as we would hope."

"Oh, no, you can't give up that easy. I'll have my secretary keep in touch with the judge's office, and we'll try again as soon as he's back in town. We'll get those two meeting each other if we have to put your grandmother in a basket and leave her on his doorstep," the attorney joked as he escorted Ida Mae to his outer office.

"Oh, by the way, do you know a character by the name of Randolph Patrick?" she asked just before turning to leave.

"No, should I?"

"I guess not; just thought I'd ask. See you in a couple weeks."

Ida Mae could not have felt more discouraged if she had gotten an Easter basket at Christmas. She had no choice but to find Rosa Lee and Mary Sue and attempt to make the most of the day. This endeavor turned out to be a minor chore for as she turned on to Main Street the ladies were standing on the corner waiting to cross. "Wait for me," she called as she pulled into a nearby parking space. The ladies spent the next several hours acting like a group of teenagers. They laughed, talked, joked and shopped in almost every store on Main Street. Rosa Lee was having the time of her life. She even seemed to enjoy being kidded about her old beau Sidney and her new-found flame, Randolph.

"How about we grab a bite to eat and hit one more store?" Ida Mae suggested. A few minutes later, she was leading them into one of the most expensive dress shops in the city. They strolled through the aisles for some time, then Ida Mae asked her grandmother to pick one she would really like.

"I think this one would really look good on me, don't you? Oh my goodness, not this one," she whispered.

"Why not?" Ida Mae asked.

Rosa Lee pointed to the price tag attached to the sleeve. "Who could afford a garment such as this, and where would I wear it?" she asked.

"I can afford it, and you can wear in your wedding," Ida Mae teased, as she took the dress from the rack and headed to the checkout counter. "When is it going to be anyway?"

"What?"

"The wedding. I was sure Randolph must have asked by now; you two have been spending a lot of time together."

"You are joking, aren't you? He hasn't even asked to hold my hand yet."

This was exactly the kind of answer the sisters hoped for, neither of them trusted this Patrick fellow and were worried their grandmother was getting much too serious about him.

"What would you like to do next?" Mary Sue asked.

"I'm really getting tired; and if you girls don't mind, I'd really like to head back to Winston. Maybe we can get an early start back to Virginia in the morning."

Chapter Eight

A WELCOMED VISITOR

The ladies remained in their jovial spirit during the ride back to Winston. Ida Mae continued teasing her grandmother about trying to find a second husband; and Mary Sue, for not yet finding her first one.

"I'm not looking," Mary Sue confessed, "but if the right one should stop by I'd lasso him before he got away."

"He may already be here, Sis," Ida Mae told her as she turned onto Chestnut Street. An old pickup truck was parked in front of their house. Attached to the truck was a trailer and on the trailer was J.D.'s Green Dragon.

Mary Sue's eyes lit up like two flashing neon signs and her smile revealed how happy she was to see him. She jumped out of Ida Mae's car and almost ran to the front porch where Jake and J.D. were sitting. "What are you doing in town, and why didn't you let me, I mean us, know you were coming?" she asked. J.D.

"I stopped to visit for a couple hours and to tell you that you'll be in Charlotte next Saturday."

"I will?"

"Remember you promised to be my biggest fan when I started racing. Well, I'll be driving in my first real stock car race next weekend in Charlotte. Some of the best known drivers around will be there including none other than Fireball himself, so the stands will be filled to capacity."

"You mean Fireball Roberts? Really?"

"The one and only, you haven't already made plans I hope."

"As a matter of fact, spring break begins next weekend; and I was planning to spend time with Mom and Dad up in the mountains."

"Tell you what. If you'll come see me race, I'll take you up there myself Sunday morning."

Mary Sue hesitated for a moment. "But, how will I get there?"

"I'll take you," Jake volunteered. "I wouldn't want to miss my brother's first race as a professional."

"Then I guess I'll have to keep my promise."

"Great, I'll call Smokey's Pit Stop right now and tell them you'll go on at eight."

"Smokey's, go on at eight, what are you talking about J.D.?"

"Oh, I must have forgot to tell you; you'll be singing on stage at the biggest nightspot in Charlotte after the race Saturday night. All the drivers will be there, and there'll be standing room only with folks wanting autographs, you know."

Mary Sue looked at her brother-in-law who appeared not to hear a word that was being said. "You knew about this all along, didn't you Jake?"

"Only for about an hour, that's when J.D. arrived," he confessed.

Mary Sue gave J.D. a quick kiss on the cheek, "If you're as good at driving as you are conniving, you'll finish an hour ahead of the rest."

"Just ten seconds ahead would make me a winner, and I have to be leaving; qualifying begins in the morning, and all the drivers have to be there."

"You're already a winner," Mary Sue told him as she stood beside the old pickup and watched him drive away. Ida Mae and Granny left the next morning for Virginia, and Mary Sue began

Granny's Justice

rehearsing for her Saturday night performance. She was grateful to J.D, and she wanted him to be as proud of her on stage as she would be of him on the track.

She and Jake rolled into Charlotte on Friday afternoon as J.D. had requested. They drove directly to the track, showed their complimentary pass at the gate and walked inside. They found their seats near the starting line just as one of the cars flew by. A few moments later, J.D came to where they were sitting.

"How did you find us so quickly?" Mary Sue asked," as another car sailed past.

"These are the seats I requested, and here are your room keys. You are registered at the Colonial Hotel, on Main Street near the end of town."

Mary Sue smiled and shook her head. "You've taken care of everything but the popcorn, haven't you, J.D?"

J.D. raised his hand and shouted at one of the vendors. "Two corns and two large drinks, please. Is there anything else, Miss?"

"You're unreal J.D."

"Oh no, I don't want you to think I'm anything special, the only thing I purchased was your refreshments. The race tickets are compliments of the racetrack owner. They are free to family members of the drivers, and your rooms were taken care of by the Pit Stop." Just then another car blew past.

"He must be doing ninety," Mary Sue said.

"Well over a hundred. I qualified at more than a hundred and twenty, and I'll start in the middle of the pack. What do you think of this place?"

"I've never seen anything like it, I can't wait for the race tomorrow."

"I hate to leave the two of you, but qualifying is almost over; and I have some minor adjustments to do on the Dragon. Stay as long as you like. I'll meet you in your hotel dining room for dinner around seven. Just for the record, Miss Duncan, it's okay if you think I'm special."

53

Jake and Mary Sue left the track shortly after the qualifying ended. They went to their rooms, relaxed for a while then got dressed for dinner. They met, as planned, in the hotel lobby an hour before time for J.D. and visited with some of the other hotel guests.

It wasn't hard to start a conversation because it seemed everyone wanted to talk about the next day's race. Fireball Roberts was by far the favorite of most of the guests although they learned he had qualified several cars behind the leaders. Some of the patrons, however, were rooting for one or more of the three rookies.

Mary Sue felt herself blush a bit and her head swelled a little when one of guests mentioned the rookies by name. "That fellow driving the car with Green Dragon written on the side appears to really know how to handle that machine, especially in the turns. He may not win, but I'll wager he'll be among the top five finishers."

Mary Sue didn't join the conversation because she knew so little about the sport, but she really enjoyed listening to their discussion, especially about the new drivers on the circuit.

J.D. made his entrance promptly at seven. He was dressed in a pair of jeans, a white pullover shirt and a leather jacket decorated with racing paraphernalia. It may not have been the formal dinner attire, but she had to admit he did look rather sharp. She was also impressed that he wanted to talk more about her during dinner than he did about racing. "Want to see the night lights of Charlotte?" he asked as they were leaving the dining room. '

Jake, realizing of course the invitation was for Mary Sue rather than him, pretended to be tired and declined. Mary Sue accepted his offer on the condition that he have her back to the hotel by midnight.

"Not one minute after," he promised as he ushered her to the parking lot and helped her into his pickup. They drove slowly down Main Street, and she listened as he told about the different bars, nightclubs, and restaurants he had visited. Most sounded rather nice, but he suggested a couple would not be suitable for a lady like her.

"What kind of lady do you think I am?" she asked.

"One who is young, innocent, beautiful, highly intelligent, and the most talented I have ever met. One who would not appreciate visiting a smoke-filled bar room where half-drunk patrons danced to loud music on the jukebox and bragged about things they had done or wanted others to believe they'd done."

"Thanks, J.D., you're sweet; and I'm glad you feel that way."

"I could have told you I've felt that way for months," he said as he pulled into the parking lot of Smokey's Pit Stop.

"Is this where I'll be performing tomorrow night?" she asked, trying to not let him know how really excited she was.

"It sure is; let's go inside."

When the doorman called J.D. by name it was obvious he was no stranger to the Pit Stop. When he opened the door allowing the couple to enter, Mary Sue was in awe. It was not difficult to realize the establishment was appropriately named. Booths simulating the interior of different model automobiles were carefully placed on a huge mirrored hardwood dance floor. Scented candles flickered in the center of each table and flashing neon lighting illuminated a large staging area with the painting of a racing pit stop in the background. Pictures of Fire Ball and other race car drivers hung on each wall, and the place was running over with racing fans.

They found a table not far from where a least half-dozen other race drivers and a host of fans were sitting. J.D and Mary Sue sipped ice-cold root beer and listened to almost everyone discuss the upcoming race. J.D was much more interested in talking to Mary Sue about what she'd been doing than who he thought might get the checkered flag.

He hadn't forgotten his promise to have her back to the hotel before midnight, and he wanted them to have some time alone. "I'd like to introduce you to someone; then if you'd like, we could go for a drive, okay?"

She smiled and gave him an approving nod just as the owner of the Pit Stop came to their table.

"Is this the lady who is going to entertain us tomorrow night?" he asked.

"She sure is, and I promise you're in for a treat. Mary Sue, meet Barney. He's the proprietor, and he's also the fellow who'll be paying for your performance."

"Pleasure to meet you, sir. Thank you for allowing me to sing for your customers tomorrow night."

"Sweetie, if your voice is as beautiful as what I'm seeing now, I'm certain I'll have to give you a bonus." He gave J.D. a quick pat on the back. "You lucky son-of-gun, whatever you guys want is on the house."

"Thanks, Barney, but we must be going. See you tomorrow night."

They were just about to leave as the band on stage began playing one of the top country hits. "Will they be accompanying me tomorrow night?" she asked.

"You got it, honey; they are without question the best country music band around."

She smiled and took J.D.'s hand, "It's not long until midnight. Don't you think we better be going?"

J.D drove to one of the scenic overlooks on the side of a mountain a few miles out of town. He parked the pickup so the lights of the city could be seen in the distance. A few other couples were also enjoying the magnificent view. There was a full moon, and a million stars blended perfectly with the lights of the city. The sound of country music being played on the radio in one of the nearby vehicles added the final touch to an almost perfect romantic setting.

"It's a much better view from over here," J.D. suggested. Mary Sue agreed as she moved closer. "I hope you don't mind," he said as her placed his arm around her shoulder.

The couple talked of growing up in the mountains of Virginia and the hardships their families had faced during and following the war and the unscrupulous manner in which her father was dismissed as a law enforcement officer and forced to take employment in the coal mines in McDowell County. They spoke about the terrible flood that caused the loss of their home as well as the homes of other families who lived along the Clinch River.

They also talked about how each of them had set out to seek a career much different than that of any of their ancestors: Mary Sue as a successful defense attorney and J.D. as a successful race car driver. They also touched on the subject of how his brother Jake, born to a family of loggers and moonshiners, could have won the heart of her sister Ida Mae, the daughter of an upstanding farming family.

It was not until the music on the radio faded into the distance they realized they were the only couple still on the mountain. The only sound that could be heard was knee-deepers in a pond somewhere nearby and a lonely whippoorwill calling to its mate. "It must be nearing midnight," Mary Sue said as she reached for J.D's. arm and looked at his watch. There was just enough light to allow her to determine it was a little past two. "Mercy, it's way past curfew, and we still have the drive back to the city, think we'll be grounded," she smiled.

"I'll never tell if you won't, " he said as he started the engine of the pickup.

When they arrived at the hotel, there was no one in the lobby. The only sign of life was the desk clerk who was barely half awake. J.D. escorted Mary Sue to her room and waited until she unlocked the door. "Good night, and thank you for a lovely evening," she said and gave him a quick kiss on the cheek.

"See you at the track tomorrow?"

"You bet."

J.D. rushed to his apartment and crashed on the sofa. He'd promised to meet his pit crew at six in the morning, and he knew he was going to be exhausted, but he had no regrets. Trying to win the affections of his favorite girl was as exciting as trying to get the checkered flag.

Mary Sue was not in the habit of being an early riser unless circumstance made it absolutely necessary. It was well after ten o'clock when she strolled into the lobby where her brother-in-law was waiting. "I thought you were going to sleep through the entire race," he teased. "Did you guys make it back by midnight as you requested?"

"Pretty close; let's get something to eat. I'm starved."

The hotel dining room was crowded with race fans, and every one was anxious to get to the track, even though the race didn't begin until noon.

Jake and Mary Sue finished their breakfast and stepped into the warm morning sunlight. They got to the track about half-hour before time for the green flag to drop and the fans were really beginning to display their excitement. The pit area was crawling with mechanics, making every needed adjustment so their cars would be in top running condition. Most of the drivers were in their full racing attire, ready to be buckled into their machines, but there was no sign of J.D.

"I wonder where he could be," Mary Sue said. "I'm sure he knows we're already here, but I haven't seen him or the Green Dragon."

"There he is," Jake answered as the Green Dragon, tires smoking, pulled from behind the wall. J.D. raised his arm and gave them the thumbs up just as a voice on the loud speakers ordered the drivers to take their starting positions.

That was the command the drivers and the fans were waiting for. The deafening roar of engines and the smell of burning rubber brought the fans to their feet. The drivers assumed their proper positions and fell in behind the pace car. They made four or five warm-up laps, and each time J.D waved as he passed. On the fifth lap, the pace car turned onto pit road, the starter waved the green flag, and the race was on. The first thirty laps were more or less routine. The drivers were testing the condition of the track and how their cars were performing. After that, the whole atmosphere changed. The drivers began passing in an attempt to move closer to the front of the pack. J.D., however, who had started fourteenth, hadn't passed a single car. Mary Sue, who knew very little about racing but knew enough about J.D to know there must be something mechanically wrong for him not to be more aggressive. He was not only failing to pass cars, he was falling back. After another ten laps, he made an unscheduled pit stop. His crew replaced both left tires. They made an adjustment to the front end, topped off his fuel tank; and in seconds, he was back on the track.

When he crossed the start-finish line next time around, he was flat out. Within a few more laps, he had regained his starting position. The track announcer made reference to how well the rookie in the Green Dragon was maneuvering around some of the veteran drivers.

"Way to go, J.D.," someone who was seated a few rows behind yelled. Mary Sue recognized Barney's voice so she stood up and waved, but he was so interested in the race he never noticed. As the competition continued, the field became more scattered; and top speeds kept increasing. There had only been two cautions brought about by minor mishaps, which gave the drivers time to refuel and get back on the track.

As the race began winding down, the fans became more involved in cheering for their favorite drivers. With only twenty laps remaining, the announcer also became more excited. "If those five cars in front continue their pace, someone will surely set a new track record," he said. This really brought the fans to their feet, and no one was cheering louder than Jake and Mary Sue, because J.D. was one of the five.

"Only fifteen laps to go," the announcer was about to say when a major pile up took place on the third turn. "There's half-dozen cars involved, and one has just gone airborne. It bounced off the wall, and it's on its side, spinning onto the grass. I believe it's the Green Dragon. Yes, it's the Hurd Boy from Virginia. Let's hope he's not badly injured. The caution flag is out, and the emergency crew is almost there." Mary Sue's heart nearly stopped. She had known it was J.D. even before the announcer, because they were in position to see the wreck as it was happening.

"Wait here," Jake told her as he headed to the fence at the edge of the track. A moment later, he realized his statement had fallen on deaf ears for Mary Sue was right on his heels. They weren't allowed any closer, because the other drivers were still moving around the track. In a matter of minutes the emergency crew had J.D. out of the Dragon. As they helped him, limping, into an ambulance he once again looked into the stands and gave thumbs up, indicating he was okay.

Jake and Mary Sue, not knowing anything else to do, waited for the track announcer to let everyone know the extent of his injuries. Shortly after the race ended, and Fire Ball Roberts headed for the winner's circle, the news they were awaiting came over the loud speakers. J.D., the announcer stated, had only suffered a mild concussion and a sprained ankle. "He may limp for a few days, but I'm sure we've not seen the last of this rookie."

Jake and Mary Sue didn't hang around for the ending celebration; instead, they headed for the nearest exit. It took nearly an hour to push their way through the excited crowd and drive to the hospital. When they reached the emergency room Mary Sue rushed to the counter in front of the nurse's desk. "Has Mr. Hurd, the race car driver, been admitted; and is he okay?" she asked.

"He's doing quite well, thank you," a voice from behind her answered.

Mary Sue knew before she turned it was J.D. He was sitting on the end of a sofa with one leg lying on a coffee table. He had a small patch over one eye and was smiling from ear to ear. She stood for a long moment with elbows propped on the counter and stared at him. She watched as he pulled himself up and limped to where she was standing.

He leaned very close, still smiling, and whispered, "You were really worried about me, weren't you?"

"I was really concerned about what you'd done to the Dragon," she grinned. "Are you ready to leave?" She turned to the nurse who returned her smile and nodded her approval.

"You bet," J.D. replied, "there's a beautiful little gal singing at the Pit Stop tonight, and I sure want to be there."

"What about the Dragon?" Jake questioned.

"My racing buddies with take care of her tonight, and I'll pick her up tomorrow."

Chapter Nine

A NIGHT AT THE PIT STOP

The excitement created by the accident allowed the afternoon to slip away faster than any of them realized. "I'll meet you guys at Smokey's," J.D. promised when they dropped him off at his apartment. "You'll barely have time to grab a bite before Mary Sue gets dressed for her performance."

"I never sing on a full stomach, but if I do well, you can buy me a burger later," she teased.

J.D. had been correct. Jake went directly to his room, spent only enough time in the shower to rid himself of the smell of oil and tire residue. In about half-hour he was back in the lobby waiting for Mary Sue. It was another fifteen minutes before his sister-in-law made an appearance; but when she did, she turned the heads of every man in the lobby. The black, rhinestone studded, vest over her white long sleeved blouse and the knee-length skirt matched her western style boots perfectly. The white gardenia pinned in her jet-black hair added the final touch to her magnificent beauty. All of her attire was compliments of her sister Ida Mae.

"She must be heading to a rodeo," someone volunteered.

"Oh, no," Jake answered, as they headed for the exit. "She'll be singing at Smokey's in about half-hour, if we make it there on time."

"Then let's go," some fellow shouted and at least twenty hotel guests headed for the parking lot.

The city was buzzing with race traffic and the five-mile drive to Smokey's was a nightmare. Barney was waiting; and when Jake pulled into the parking lot ten minutes before eight, they each breathed a sigh of relief. Mary Sue leaped from the car and started to explain why she was so late, but Barney interrupted.

"I know," he said, "come with me." He ushered her through a side door into a small room where a young man was waiting. She didn't know until moments later the room was adjacent to the stage or that the young man was the leader of the band.

"What are the titles of your first three numbers?" he asked.

She immediately gave him the titles of three top-ten country hits and noticed he looked somewhat surprised. "Are those okay?" she asked

"We'll see," he said. "When you hear Barney introduce you, step through this door and you'll be in full view of our audience. My band has never accompanied anyone before without rehearsing; I sure hope this goes okay," he added, and was gone.

Almost simultaneously she heard Barney's announcement. "Let's make welcome our sensational country entertainer for the evening, Miss Mary Sue Duncan."

"I hope he's not disappointed," she mumbled, as she stepped onto the stage. To her surprise the entire place had taken on a new appearance. What had been the stage backdrop when she was there before was now unfurled and the dance floor was twice the size as it had been. The band started playing the introduction to one of Kitty Wells' top hits, and she let go with all that was in her. By the end of the first verse, the dance floor was crowded. She turned to the bandleader and was amazed that his somber appearance was gone. He smiled, winked, and she read his lips when he mouthed, "Wow!"

After finishing the other two songs she'd picked, she and the bandleader bonded as if they had performed together for ages.

Each time she announced the title of her next number, the band began playing. Sometimes the applause would begin before she'd finished the last few words of her song. She sang non-stop for the next forty-five minutes, then Barney came on stage and joined her in front of the microphone.

"Wasn't I right? Is she not a singing sensation?" He hesitated until the applause ended. "How long have you been singing?" he asked.

"As long as I can remember," she answered as she looked over the audience in hopes of seeing J.D.. Jake was seated almost directly in front of the stage; and she knew if he were there, that's where he would be. She answered a few more of Barney's questions then turned to leave the stage. She was honored when the audience began shouting "more, more, more," but she was anxious to learn what Jake knew about J.D.

The cries ceased when Barney told them she would return after a short intermission.

"A large glass of iced tea," she told the waitress who was standing beside Jake's table. "What's happened to J.D?" was her question to Jake.

"Not a thing, I'm just fine." J.D. answered.

"Where have you been?" Mary Sue asked.

"Well it's like this, I was a bit late leaving my apartment; then I blew the left front tire on my pickup. It took a few minutes for me to hail a taxi."

"And then, what happened?" Jake asked, sensing there was something more his brother wanted to add.

"The taxi blew the tire on the right front, so I just decided with that kind of luck I'd walk the last few blocks."

"With a crippled leg?" Mary Sue questioned.

"No, honey, I left it back where I started walking, but I was right. You do worry about me."

"You jerk," she smiled. "Have a seat and help me drink this tea."

They talked and laughed about J.D.'s bad luck as patrons interrupted asking for Mary Sue's autograph. She didn't mind and was really delighted when some of the articles she signed already bore the signatures of one or more of the race car drivers. Their next interruption was Barney welcoming her back on stage for her next set. "What great entertainment we've had this evening from the beautiful young lady who hails from the mountains of Southwest Virginia. Now, let's make the applause so loud Miss Duncan can't say no when we invite her back," he said. Barney needed to say no more, for as she began her next number the applause could not have been more gratifying if Kitty Wells herself had been on stage. She sang for another half-hour before saying good night. The highlight of the evening was when she dedicated her final song to her best friend and magnificent race car driver, also from the mountains of Virginia, Mr. J.D. Hurd.

The compliments from the audience was heartwarming, and the reviews from the band was simply unreal. But the one she most cherished was the one from J.D. "If you had sounded better, you'd had to have the voice of an angel."

"Was I really that good?" she asked.

"You really were."

"Then buy me dinner; I'm hungry," she joked.

"Anything on the menu; and if I recall the last time we were together, you were hungry. How will I ever keep you fed?" He was almost sorry for his last comment because he was afraid it might sound as if he were taking something for granted.

Jake, J.D. and Mary Sue each consumed a marvelous steak dinner, compliments of the owner, and then drove to J.D.'s apartment. "When they pulled into the parking lot J.D.'s pickup was already there. "How did that happen?" Jake asked.

"Oh, it's great to have friends at the track," and after hesitating a moment, "and on stage," he added.

"We'll be heading back to Winston early in the morning, but we'll see you again real soon I hope?" Jake asked.

"You can count on that big brother. It took a great deal of work to rebuild the Dragon into one that would qualify for racing and looks like I'll have it to do again."

That brought a warm smile from Mary Sue. She was about to ask him to give up the sport of racing, but the words stuck in her throat.

"I'll call you," he whispered. In a moment they were gone.

Chapter Nine

GOODBYE TO WINTER

The early spring days had driven away the dismal gray haze of winter that had hung over the mountains of Russell County. As new life sprang forth with the sight of Easter lilies, daffodils, and crimson pods on redbud trees, Rosa Lee grew restless. Her feeling of usefulness dwindled with each passing day. On the farms where she'd spent most of her life, Spring was a time for planting, painting, and helping with minor repairs brought about by the harsh winds of Winter.

The place they now lived could be measured in feet and inches instead of acres. The house was so small Mary Ellen needed no help keeping it in order. The responsibility of being sheriff kept Ira busy chasing criminals at least twelve hours a day, and the teenage twins kept busy chasing squirrels, rabbits, or the young ladies who lived in the community. That left Rosa Lee with nothing but time on her hands, and she was determined not to use it sitting on the front porch watching the grass grow. She'd only been home for three days, and she was already getting bored. She'd let Ida Mae go back to Winston without her, and she was having second thoughts about that! At least in the city, there was always something to do; Randolph would see to that.

Then early one morning she got an exciting idea. She decided she would go visit Gertie. They could sit on the banks of the Clinch, gossip and fish all day. Even if the fish weren't biting, they could count frogs, turtles, and train cars moving on the tracks that ran along side the river. The idea was so exciting, she could hardly wait for Ira to come home and drive her the twenty miles or so to Cleveland; and that's exactly what she had him do. She insisted he let her out in town so she could walk the remaining three-quarter mile along the tracks to where her friend lived. It was nearing dusk, but Ira was not about to argue with his mother because he knew he couldn't win. He did, however, sit in the squad car and wait until she was out of sight.

As Rosa Lee walked, she began recalling the days a short time earlier when her family lived on the river. The remains of their home that the flood had destroyed were only a few feet ahead. She paused a while to dwell on the good times the family had enjoyed, the bad times they had endured, and what had brought them there in the first place. One of the best times had been spent with her friend Gertie. She decided she had best keeping walking if she was going to get there before dark.

When she reached Gertie's house, there no sign of life. The last remnants of daylight were fading, and night was closing in. She called out for her friend but got no answer. She pushed gently on the front door, and it swung partially open, but there was no sound from inside. The night creatures were beginning to make themselves known, so Rosa Lee sat in Gertie's porch swing and listened to their chirping, croaking, and splashing while trying to decide what she should do next. Hundreds of fireflies emerged from the banks of the river and seemed fascinated by their own reflection in the water.

Sometime later, a movement a short ways down the tracks drew Rosa Lee's attention and caused her to smile. It was Bingo, Gertie's golden retriever, trotting along a few feet ahead his mistress. Gertie was ambling along as if she didn't have a care in the world, her cane pole in one hand and a dozen nice horneyheads on a string in the other. She was humming a tune Rosa Lee recognized as one found in their church hymnal, and Bingo appeared to be enjoying every note. It was so near dark, Gertie wasn't aware there was anyone within a mile of her place. Even Bingo, who was in dog years much older than his mistress, wasn't even aware they had company. Gertie was wearing her normal fishing attire, a brown plaid skirt over a pair of denim pants with the legs tucked into the top of her four-buckle rubber boots.

"Nice catch," Rosa Lee said when Gertie was just a few feet in front of her. Gertie was so startled she let out a yell that silenced the frogs. She dropped her cane pole and threw her catch into the air. The fish landed right in Rosa Lee's lap.

"I'd rather have them fried," Rosa Lee said as she got up and threw her arms around Gertie.

"Rosa Lee Duncan! You scared the next three years growth right out of me!"

"Gertie, you haven't grown any in the last decade, but I am sorry I scared you."

"How did you get here anyway, hobo a train?"

"Oh no, Ira dropped me off up town; and I walked down the railroad."

"At this time of night?"

"What about you, you're walking the tracks at night?"

"Yes, but I've got old Bingo. He'll take care of me."

Rosa Lee was pretty sure that if she yelled boo loud enough Bingo would probably run under the porch. However she was glad Gertie felt she had some type of security.

Gertie pointed to the bag sitting at Rosa Lee's feet, "This means you come to stay a few days, I hope."

"Only if you have another fishing pole; remember I lost mine in the flood."

"A brand spanking new one I've been saving for just such a special occasion; you can try it out tomorrow." She picked up Rosa

Lee's bag and said, "Come on in, Honey; you're just in time for supper. We'll have planned over's tonight and will feast on hornies tomorrow."

"You mean left overs?" Rosa Lee asked.

"No, Honey, I mean planned overs. I cooked a big meal yesterday, ate all I could hold, and planned to eat on the remainder for the next few days. Come on in, and let's get started."

Rosa Lee followed Gertie inside and was about to say she wasn't really hungry, when Gertie lifted the lid from a kettle of her famous homemade beef stew. She immediately decided some comments were best kept quiet..

"Pull up a chair, and get me caught up on the world's happenings while I warm our supper."

Rosa Lee watched as Gertie lifted one eye on her wood burning cook stove and shoved two or three pieces of dry kindling inside. Bingo curled up near the wood box that would soon be the warmest place in the room. Rosa Lee scooted her cane bark-bottomed straight-back chair a little closer to the stove and leaned back against the wall. It was not really cold, but the warmth of the stove felt good to her body, and Gertie's friendship felt good to her soul. She listened to the crackling of the firewood as she recalled the time Gertie took her family under her wing. It had been during one of the most devastating disasters to ever hit the county. She'd shared her home, given them food and shelter, and asked nothing in return. Rosa Lee was about to become lost in her memory of that awful time when Gertie interrupted.

"It'll be ready in a jiffy," she said as she sat two pint-sized bowls on the red and white-checkered oilcloth. Three-quarters of a large pone of cornbread followed and then came two ice-cold glasses of buttermilk. Five minutes later the bowls were filled with Gertie's own steaming hot beef stew and the feast began.

The two old friends talked and ate for the better part of an hour. Each time Rosa Lee's bowl neared the half-empty mark, Gertie would fill it again. And, each time she refilled the bowl, another chunk of wood went into the stove. By the time their meal was finished, the kitchen was toasty warm; and Rosa Lee was so full she could hardly breathe.

Gertie scrapped the remains of what was left in their bowls into a pan a few inches from Bingo's head. She added a generous portion from the stew kettle and gave him a pat on the head as he began to devour his dinner. "Bingo is getting old," she offered, "but he sure is good company."

"Ever think of getting married again?" Rosa Lee asked.

Gertie hesitated for a moment pretending to put some thought into Rosa Lee's question. "Yes, I distinctly remember one day shortly after Herman passed. I was having very little luck digging red worms out by the hog pen when I began thinking how nice it would be if I had a strong fellow to help me around here. But you know, the very next spade full of soil I turned yielded me enough bait for the next day's fishing trip, and I haven't entertained the thought of getting hitched since. Don't tell me you're contemplating tying the knot again."

"I must admit, I have given it some thought lately; but not seriously, you understand."

"Has your old beau, The Judge, already asked you to get married? If so, he sure works fast; you haven't been down where he lives but a little while."

"Oh no, I haven't even spoken to Sidney, but you know there is more than one duck on the pond."

"My goodness, Rosa Lee, it sounds like you are really serious about catching yourself a duck, or drake, or whatever the case may be."

Rosa Lee offered to clean the dishes but Gertie would not hear of it. "Just continue telling me about Ida Mae, Jake, Mary Sue, J.D. and life in the city, and I won't sleep a wink if I don't hear more about this other duck you mentioned.

"I do hope you'll stay for a few days Rosa Lee, so much has happened since you moved away; and, by the way, the fishing has been great. Oh! That reminds me I still have to clean those hornies."

Rosa Lee sat by the stove while Gertie prepared her day's catch with all the skill of an experienced butcher.

"There's another matter that's been bothering me," Rosa Lee confessed. "Ira tries not to worry me or Mary Ellen but she knows some bad things have been happening and she believes Baxter is to blame."

"That's odd. I thought he'd left for places unknown."

"Exactly what he wants everyone to think, but Mary Ellen believes he's still around, using some sort of disguise. She's certain he has a police radio in his possession because he seems to know where Ira and his deputies are at all times. There was a dead animal placed on our porch, grease put on the door handles of Ira's cruiser, and prank calls coming in at all hours. These are the things she knows and she's certain there are others Ira won't tell her about."

"What about the family who leased Baxter's farm? Surely they would know if he is back in the area."

"The Sutters? Ira has questioned them on more than one occasion, and they swore they haven't seen him since the day he left the county. They tend to keep to themselves and have little to do with any of the people who live around them. But, you must realize these people are not the most intelligent or over ambitious folks around. The lady of the house appears to be a hard worker, but her better half is quite the opposite. I've heard he complains of some health problem constantly and insists he is unable to work. According to those who are in the know, his two overgrown redneck sons have inherited his health problems.

"The cornfields haven't yet been plowed, none of the fences damaged by the winter storms have been mended and Baxter's cattle don't appear to be suffering from being overfed."

"What have they done all winter?"

"Now, that's easy to determine; all four sides of the corncrib and one end of the barn is covered with muskrat, coon, or beaver pelts. There's even two fox hides nailed to the side of their outhouse. They're real outdoorsmen, I guess; but anyway, they must be telling the truth about Baxter. If he'd been around, he'd at least had them repair the roof that's half blown off the tool shed. Anyway, enough about the Sutters, I've just got to find a way to catch Baxter before something really bad happens to Ira or one of us."

"Appears you have a problem we both need to work on. Let's turn in for the night and we'll get started figuring that out in the morning."

"I know between the two of us we can come up with a plan to get to the truth of Baxter's whereabouts and find out more about the Sutter's. Good night, Gertie"

Chapter Ten

A DAY OF DECISION

Rosa Lee spent the next two weeks with Gertie. Most of their time was spent on the banks of the Clinch. They'd get up early in the morning, eat breakfast, pack a lunch and head to the river. They'd stay until nightfall unless a springtime thunderstorm drove them in or they had to leave in time to gather enough bait for their trip the next day.

The ladies fished every day except Sunday. Gertie may have had her share of shortcomings, but missing church was not one of them. On the Sabbath, she laid aside her fishing gear, dressed in her finest clothes, and walked the three-quarter mile to the Baptist church as she had done for as long as anyone could remember. She had been given the privilege of ringing the church bell when she was not yet five years old, and she'd performed her duty well for more than sixty years.

Rosa Lee was glad for the opportunity to accompany Gertie to Sunday Services. She'd be able to see some of the people she hadn't seen since shortly after the flood. And, although she enjoyed fishing, she was not as obsessed with the sport as was Gertie.

Gertie was born near the banks of the Tug River, in a house similar to where she now lived; and no one was more knowledgeable about fishing these waters than she. Being an only child was to her one of life's greatest blessings. She loved her parents dearly and being an only child meant she did not have to share them with anyone. Her daddy was her hero; he'd let her help with whatever he was doing—working the garden, gathering eggs, painting the house, or hoeing corn, even if he had to replant some of the plants she mistakenly took for weeds.

Her daddy had been an early riser, and that suited Gertie just fine. No use letting the day go by lying in bed he would say. If you get started with your chores early, you could always go fishing in the evening. He insisted that was when fishing was at its best.

Rosa Lee and Gertie began their trek to the church just as the sun was beginning to burn away the morning fog. Many of the insects that lived along the river were exercising their wings. Such was the case with one mosquito that lingered an instant too long near the surface of the water. A large bass leaped from the depths of the river and like a bolt of lightning the mosquito was gone.

"Did you see that?" Rosa Lee asked. "I'll bet that bass was twenty inches long."

Gertie smiled. "Nearer two feet I'd say. I'll bring my rule in the morning, and we'll see which of us is right."

The ladies strolled along the tracks talking about what they should use in order to tease that big fish into taking their hook. In a little while, they reached the Baptist church near the center of town. Gertie went inside, and Rosa Lee sat on a bench near the edge of the curb in front of the building. In a few moments the beckoning call of church bells began ringing. A couple minutes later the toll of the bells hushed, and Gertie came outside and sat beside Rosa Lee and looked at her watch. "The pastor will be here in precisely eight minutes," she said. "He's always the first to arrive at exactly thirty minutes before church time, and it's been that way for years."

Rosa Lee was about to make some remark about the pastor just as Deputy Barton pulled in front of where they were seated. He was in full uniform and driving his police cruiser so the ladies knew right away he was not there to attend worship services.

"You must be taking care of some mighty important police business if you're not attending church this morning, Howard," Gertie said.

Deputy Barton got out of his car and came and sat on the bench beside Rosa Lee. He took her hand and cleared his throat a couple of times before he was able to compose himself enough to speak. "Ira's been hurt," he said, as he felt Rosa Lee's hand begin to tremble.

"An accident?" she asked.

Howard shook his head. "There was some type of an explosion, and we're sure it was no accident."

"Tell me the truth, Howard; Is he alive?"

"He's alive, but he is in bad shape. I'll tell you all about it on the way to the hospital."

"Baxter!" Granny shouted. "He'll curse the day he ever heard the name Rosa Lee Duncan!"

"We don't know for sure he was responsible, but you better believe if he is in this part of the country, we'll track him down."

Howard opened the door to his cruiser; and as Rosa Lee got in, she beckoned to Gertie. "Please come with us." Her friend slid in beside her and whispered; "You know we're in this together."

The deputy turned on all his emergency lights and sped away as the church crowd began to gather.

"Tell us how it happened," Rosa Lee said.

"If you remember," Howard began, "last night was the date for the annual spring dance at the Star Light; and, as usual almost everyone for miles around was there. Ira, two other deputies and I were on duty. I parked my cruiser at one end of the lot; Ira parked his at the other, and the other deputies parked near the front entrance. The band was great; the crowd was orderly and there appeared to be no sign of trouble so Ira allowed the other deputies to mark off at midnight.

"At exactly one a.m. the dispatcher reported a break-in at a service station in town. Most of the crowd had already left the dance so I decided to follow Ira to investigate the break-in. Within five minutes of our leaving, a ball of fire erupted from under the hood of Ira's car. He veered off the shoulder of the road and over an embankment. He would have gone into a creek had it not been for a large oak tree.

"I reported the incident to our dispatcher and was by the sheriff's side within seconds. The hood of his car was completely blown away, and the windshield was shattered. I pulled him from the car and waited for the ambulance, which was there within about half-hour. I stayed on scene until the other deputies got there and then went directly to the hospital. It was well after sun-up before the doctors let us know he was going to recover. By that time, every available law enforcement officer from every surrounding county was there to help capture who ever was responsible."

"How badly was he hurt?" Rosa Lee asked.

"He had a really bad cut on the side of his head but I was able to stop the bleeding. I won't lie to you Rosa Lee, he was unconscious so other than the injury to the head I can't say. But the doctors said he would be all right but he'd have to take it easy for a few weeks."

"Do you have any information about who did this to him, as if we didn't already know?"

"The only lead we have is that someone noticed an older model pickup with Tennessee license plates number TK0-123 pulling away from the Star Light just moments before the call about the break-in was reported. Incidentally, there was nothing happening at the service station. It was simply a phony report to get the sheriff in his automobile at exactly the right moment. We have determined it was some sort of timing device, but that's all we know at this time. There are dozens of officers looking for the pickup as we speak. Ira's cruiser is locked away in a body shop in town and the state police will begin examining every inch of it right away.

"Our officers are questioning the folks who might have been leaving the dance at about the time Ira and I were leaving. It was one of them who saw the pickup. The only thing they could tell us about the driver was that he was wearing a large felt hat that hid his entire head. The most frustrating fact is that whoever is committing these acts knows where Ira is at all times."

When Howard turned onto the street leading to the hospital at least twenty police cars came into view. Gertie leaned closer to Rosa Lee and whispered, "I guess these fellows are pretty good, but I think they might need a little help, don't you?"

The deputy parked at the emergency room entrance where several officers were gathered. A state police sergeant opened the door for the two ladies and escorted them to a small waiting room where Mary Ellen sat, anxiously waiting news from the O. R.

Chapter Eleven

A SLOW RECOVERY

The next few days were a nightmare for the Duncan family. Ira was still in a coma; the officers were no closer to solving the mystery of who had planted the explosive device in his car, and Rosa Lee's patience was wearing thin.

Mary Ellen, the girls, and John Robert were staying in a hotel just two blocks from the hospital, at the expense of the county, of course. Rosa Lee was seeing the twins off to school each day and then there was nothing left for her to do but think. She was certain Baxter was responsible for what had happened to Ira and she was determined to help prove it. She tried not to show how worried she was when the twins were home; but when they were in school, she thought she'd lose her sanity. A member of the family called each morning and night to report Ira's condition, but there was never any improvement. Her emotions were so mixed she spent half her time praying for her son and the remainder cursing Baxter.

Howard Barton, who was now in charge, kept her informed about every lead but not one of them proved to be helpful. Every deputy was working almost around the clock but to no avail. It seemed as if whoever planted the explosive had vanished from the face of the earth and taken the pick-up with them.

By the end of the week, worry and depression had almost taken its toll on Rosa Lee when suddenly there appeared a glimmer of hope. She was sitting in the porch swing, so lost in her thoughts she was not aware there was an automobile stopped near the yard gate until John Robert blew the horn.

Rosa Lee jumped to her feet and was about to bounce off the porch when suddenly she froze. The back seat of John Robert's car was filled with flowers. "Please don't tell me he's . . . " Before she could finish speaking, John Robert interrupted, "Dad's coming around. He opened his eyes, asked for Mom, and whispered, 'I'm okay.'

"The doctor was in his room almost immediately. He checked his vitals and for the first time admitted he had been deeply concerned, but now he was sure that Daddy would make a complete recovery."

The twins came running from somewhere around back just in time to hear their big brother's comments. "What are you doing with all that funeral stuff if daddy is all right?" Kervin asked.

John Robert didn't know whether to laugh or cry.

"These are not for his funeral. They're from all his friends who were praying for him to get better. Help me carry them inside," he said and he opened the trunk revealing even more of potted good wishes. "You can take care of these," he said to Granny as he handed her a huge bundle of get-well cards. "They were coming so fast there was scarcely room left for Daddy."

Rosa Lee was so relieved she was beside herself. She had arranged and rearranged the potted flowers along the edge of the porch for at least the third time when another surprise came into view—Ida Mae and Gertie.

"Would you mind putting up with a friend for a few days?" Gertie questioned.

"Just you try to leave," Rosa Lee answered. She threw her arms around Gertie and for the first time since she had received news about Ira, she let go. She buried her face on Gertie's shoulder and allowed the tears to flow. Gertie allowed her a moment to compose herself before announcing she had brought along a friend.

"Who?" Rosa Lee asked, unable to see anyone else.

"Come along, boy," Gertie yelled.

Bingo stood up in the back and waited for Ida Mae to open the door. He then made a beeline for the twins. "I knew he would remember the boys; hope you don't mind, he can sleep on your porch."

"No way," Kervin volunteered, "Bingo can sleep with me, and Kevin can sleep on the porch."

* * * * * *

Ira began improving more and more each day. The girls went back to Winston, John Robert returned to his job on the coast and Gertie and Bingo settled in with Granny and the twins. Rosa Lee felt safer with Gertie on board. Howard or one of the other deputies was usually not far away, but she never knew what Baxter or one of his cronies might try next. Only she knew she had been sleeping with Ira's service revolver under her pillow each night.

Rosa Lee's days of waiting for Ira to recover had become much easier with her friend Gertie to keep her company; but still, she could not wait for him to come home. He was to be discharged just any time, and she could hardly wait. She enjoyed the time she spent with Gertie but she was getting restless. It was a beautiful Monday morning and she felt bad she could not think of a way to entertain her guest. "What would you like to do today?" she asked.

"Let's go for a walk," Gertie suggested. "It's a wonderful day for walking and Bingo and I never miss a chance to walk at least a mile on the railroad tracks on days like this. Right Bingo?"

Bingo jumped to his feet as if he knew exactly what Gertie had said.

"Sorry we don't have any tracks; but if you don't mind a little dust we sure have miles of gravel road."

"Mind, are you kidding? Let's get going."

The ladies began their stroll in a westerly direction that took them past the Baxter farm. The Sutter family were busy doing what they do best, sitting on the porch watching the grass grow, except Otis, the youngest and most energetic of the clan. Otis was down below the springhouse picking creasy greens and pitching them into a water bucket. When he saw the ladies coming, he stopped what he was doing, sat down on the bucket, and waited for them to get close enough to start a conversation.

"Morning girls, my name's Otis; what's your'n? Air you the ones that lives in that little house down yonder, the ones got runned off afore we moved in?"

The ladies could determine right away that the days Otis spent in the school system was not as the superintendent. Not wanting to be rude and at the same time not wanting to get into a lengthy discussion, Rosa Lee told him her name and kept walking.

"Fine looking dog you got there. Is he a good hunter?"

Rosa Lee couldn't resist, "No Otis, he was raised on the banks of the river. He don't hunt, he just fishes."

"Oh," was all Otis could muster. Then after a moment "Me and Mommy, my older brother, and my old man are going to town after while. Can we bring you women back some'um?" When he got no answer, he just sat on the bucket of greens and watched until they were out of sight.

The ladies strolled along the graveled road for about another hour, stopping occasionally to exchange a word or two with a neighbor. "It must be nearing the noon hour," Gertie reasoned. "It's getting really warm for this time of year, old Bingo is beginning to pant. Don't you think we ought to start back?"

Rosa Lee was also getting tired so she quickly agreed. They were almost back home when a relative of Bingo's worst enemies appeared from out of nowhere and raced across the road in front of them.

"Oh, my goodness, the race is on now!" Gertie yelled, as Bingo tore out like he'd been shot out of a cannon.

"What do you mean 'the race is on'? I thought Bingo was too old to go chasing anything but his tail."

"You're right Rosa Lee, everything but groundhogs. Ever notice Bingo has one ear that's is somewhat shorter than the other?"

"Now that you mentioned it, his head did look a might unbalanced."

"Well, let me tell you how it happened. When Bingo was little feller, he followed his mother everywhere she went, trying to learn how to be a big dog, I suppose. Anyway, it was on a beautiful Sunday afternoon right after I'd gotten home from church and finished lunch that Bingo, Wilabee, that was Bingo's mommy, and I were relaxing in the back yard. Suddenly one of the biggest, fattest groundhogs I had ever seen scampered under the garden fence and began helping himself to some of the vegetables. As you can imagine Wilabee was to have no part of that. She didn't even yelp, but she was headed for the garden in a flash, and Bingo was right on her heels. Wilabee nailed that fat rascal by the back of the neck, and the groundhog nailed Bingo by the ear. It was a full two minutes before I could tell which one was going to give up first. At last, it was evident the groundhog had lost the fight, but Bingo had lost the tip of his ear. To this day I don't think he ever let very many escape."

The entire time Gertie was telling about Bingo's encounter with his first whistle pig, he was giving full chase after the one now in question.

"In his younger days that rascal would already be history; but Bingo is catching up, right Rosa Lee?"

Bingo was still a few feet behind when the groundhog disappeared into a hole under a board on the side of the barn on Baxter's farm. A moment later Bingo was also inside the barn.

"No use us trying to call him off," Gertie said. "Might as well sit for a spell and wait until Bingo finishes the fight or gets so tired he has to give up."

The ladies waited several minutes, but Bingo didn't seem to be engaged in any real scuffle; nor did it sound as if he was anywhere near giving up.

"I better go see what's got him so frustrated, or we might be here all day," Gertie suggested. She crossed the fence and walked to the side of the barn, placed one eye over a knothole and peered inside. She turned back to Rosa Lee, displaying a big smile, and motioned for her to come see. Rosa Lee joined her and took a turn at the knothole. What she witnessed was enough to make almost anyone laugh out loud. Bingo had the groundhog at bay in the cab of an old '49 Chevy pickup truck. The furry animal would stand in the seat on the driver's side and peer out the window while Bingo clawed at the door trying to get inside. It would then move to the opposite end of the seat and wait for Bingo to begin clawing at that door. The groundhog seemed rather calm, but poor Bingo was going out of his mind.

The ladies enjoyed the show for a little while before deciding to give both critters some relief. Gertie tugged at a loose board until they were able to squeeze inside. "I'll hold Bingo while you give the rodent a reprieve," she told Rosa Lee.

Rosa Lee opened the door on the driver's side just as the groundhog scampered through a hole in the floorboard and disappeared under a pile of loose hay. She was about to close the door when she noticed a Tennessee license plate lying on the floor of the pickup. It was partially hidden by a large dirty felt hat.

"Hold on to your dog, and let's get out of here," Rosa Lee said in a tone of voice that was more demand rather than a request. "I know who hurt Ira, and I've got to call Howard."

Gertie didn't take time to ask questions; she tightened her grip on Bingo's collar, and followed Rosa Lee out of the barn. They were almost back to the road when the Sutters turned into the lane leading up to the farmhouse. Otis looked straight at them, but this time he was not so friendly.

"What air you women doing on this place?" he wanted to know.

Rosa Lee was about to make up some sort of answer, but Gertie beat her to the draw. "My dog, Bingo, chased a copperhead under the fence, and we were afraid he might get bit so we went after him."

"Oh, I thought you might have been up to the barn."

"Shut up, Otis," Old Man Sutter ordered. "Did the dog get the copperhead, Ma,am?"

Rosa Lee didn't volunteer an answer, she decided it was Gertie's lie she'd let her tell it as big as she had a mind too.

"No, sir, it slithered under that pile of rocks."

"You don't say," he answered and drove on up the lane.

Rosa Lee could hardly wait to get to the telephone. She called Ira's office and gave orders to the dispatcher to have Deputy Barton to contact her at once. "Tell him it is of the utmost importance."

"He is somewhere in your area as we speak, Mrs. Duncan. I haven't heard from him for a while but I will get your message to him at once."

Within an hour Howard was answering the call. Rosa Lee hurriedly filled him in on the details of her discovery and was disappointed that he was unable to go after the Sutters at once.

"We must go about this in the proper way," he assured her. "If the Sutters are to blame for this crime, which in fact they are, you can bet Baxter is behind the whole scheme. Come with me to the magistrate's office, and we will secure a search warrant. I'll bring more deputies back with us, and we will take what you've found as evidence. We'll have them locked up before sundown."

Rosa Lee left Gertie in charge of the twins and headed to the magistrate's office. Obtaining the warrant was much easier than she had expected; the magistrate was as anxious as she to see the guilty parties brought to justice.

As promised every available deputy accompanied Howard to the Baxter farm. They planned to swarm the premises before the Sutters knew what was happening. But, to their surprise none of the Sutter clan appeared to be upset when presented with the warrant. In fact, they appeared to be more than willing to cooperate.

The officers set about trying to find the licenses plates, the felt hat, or anything else that might incriminate the Sutters; but not one single piece of evidence could be found. She could hardly believe what she was hearing when Howard told her what had happened and that he was compelled to apologize to the Sutters.

"I know they're guilty," he told her, "but we don't dare make an arrest without enough evidence to make the charges hold up in court."

"I know you're right, Howard; but I won't give up until I see Baxter and the Sutters behind bars."

"Ira will be home soon, so please let us handle this matter, Granny," Howard pleaded.

Rosa Lee smiled and thanked him.

Chapter Twelve

BACK TO WINSTON

The thought of having Baxter slip through their hands was almost more than Rosa Lee could handle. She knew now that he was using the Sutters to do his dirty work; and each time one of them would go by, the hair would stand up on the back of her neck.

Ira was home making a remarkable recovery; Gertie had gone back to her home on the river, and she had Howard's assurance he would not give up until everyone involved was made to pay for what they had done to the sheriff. So, once again, Rosa Lee felt the need to move back to Winston. A phone call to Ida Mae was all it took.

The girls loved their granny and were happy to have her back, but they were becoming concerned about her involvement with Patrick. They had hoped a few weeks back home would lessen her feelings about him, but they soon learned that was not the case. She had only been in Winston two days when he came calling and, of course, he was sporting another new Caddy. Rosa Lee was relaxing on the front porch with Mary Sue, Ida Mae and Jake.

"This is a pleasant surprise," Randolph said as he got out of the car. "I just stopped by to find out when you were going to be back in the city."

"Miss me, did you?" Granny asked, giggling like a teenager hoping to be asked out on her first date.

Randolph stuttered for a moment and finally managed to explain he had a really good deal in the making; then asked if she would like to go for a drive.

Ida Mae was not about to let an opportunity like this one pass. Before Rosa Lee could answer, she insisted that instead of a drive, he join them for refreshments so they could get better acquainted.

Unable to gracefully decline, he accepted.

"Granny, won't you get Randolph a glass of tea?" she suggested.

Rosa Lee was barely out of hearing distance when again Ida Mae seized the opportunity to learn all she could about her granny's car salesman buddy.

"Tell us more about this good deal," she said.

"Beg your pardon? Oh, the car deal. We're about to close the deal on two more new Caddies up near Galax. If we finalize the sale, we'll have to deliver them day after tomorrow."

"Galax, that's in Virginia isn't it?" Mary Sue questioned.

"Just barely."

"You deliver most of the automobiles you sell?" Jake asked.

"Oh, yes, most all the sales we make are to repeat customers. Nearly all live in Florida or Southern Georgia and have summer homes here in the mountains. They just call and order the automobile they desire; and in a matter of days, we have it sitting in their driveway. How's that for service?"

"Far out." Jake offered, just as Granny reappeared with a large frosty glass of iced tea.

Randolph stayed until almost sundown; but at times he did not seem to be very comfortable, especially when some of the questions that were asked were about his line of work. At the first opportunity, he remembered something he had forgotten to do and begged to be excused. "I'll call you tomorrow if we make the sale, Rosa Lee; and you can let me know if you'd like to drive one of the Caddies."

"Sure thing," she told him and followed him to his automobile.

"There's something really fishy about that guy," Jake whispered.

* * * * * *

Rosa Lee was dressed long before Randolph was scheduled to arrive. She slipped out to the front porch, careful not to wake anyone, and waited while she enjoyed the beautiful sunrise. She was anxious to assist Randy in closing what he described as one of his most profitable deals and even more excited about earning her very first employment check. She could hardly believe she was going to be paid for doing something she enjoyed so much. She listened to the chirping of the baby wrens nesting in the newly budding magnolia trees. She imagined they were encouraging their parents who were scampering about on the lawn searching for their first feast of the day.

As the morning wore on and the other members of the family began to move about, she became concerned that Randolph was later than he promised. She was to follow him to her favorite restaurant where they'd first met and deliver a new car to one of his repeat customers. He was to be paid in cold hard cash, and one hundred dollars of that was to be hers. Then, as an added bonus, he promised to buy her the biggest breakfast on the menu and take her on to visit his home in Bland County.

When the grandfather clock in the hallway struck the seventh time, she realized something was not as it should be. Randy was always right on schedule. She sat very still hoping no one would discover she had not already left because she had told everyone of her plans. But, as she sat daydreaming about how she was going to spend her first bit of income Mary Sue stepped from along side the porch.

"Granny, I thought you were already gone."

Rosa Lee was so startled her first words were, "I'll just put it all in the bank."

"Sounds good to me Granny, but I didn't know your ship had come in"

Rosa Lee had not told anyone she was to be paid for every delivery. She didn't want to explain her comment to Mary Sue just now either; but she knew she needed to offer some sort of explanation. She was about to do just that as Randolph pulled to the curb. "Sorry I'm late, but we must be going," he said as he got out of the car and rushed to open the passenger door for Rosa Lee. As they sped away it was easy to tell he was in a great rush.

"Why are you so late?" she asked, knowing they were to meet the customer at nine o'clock sharp.

Randolph hesitated for a long moment. "Just trying to close on another deal," he mumbled.

"Are you sure you're all right? You look kind of pale."

"I simply don't trust that fellow," Ida Mae said as she joined her sister on the porch and watched as the Cadillac rounded the corner. "I can't put my finger on what's really going on, but I'm afraid our grandmother is in for a great disappointment."

"All the more reason we should not give up on getting her and Sidney back together," Mary Sue suggested.

Randolph drove to the same parking lot as before. He parked beside another Cadillac and handed Rosa Lee the keys. "Just follow me. We don't want to be late so please keep up."

She followed Randolph's car out of the city at which time he started driving at a higher rate of speed than he had ever driven before. Rosa Lee stayed right on his rear bumper because she had mastered her driving ability quite well, and the new car rode as if it was floating on air. In little over an hour, they were nearing the Virginia state line. Randolph pulled onto the side of the highway, came back to the automobile Rosa Lee was driving and got inside. "I think my car is overheating, I'm going to stop at the Esso station up ahead and have the mechanic check it out. You're only twenty minutes away so you'll have to go on without me. Okay?"

"Not a problem. What am I doing when I get there?"

"Go inside, order something to eat and wait for our customer if he's not already there. His name is Grady. He's a short stocky gentleman with graying hair and a mustache. I should be along right away; but if he gets there before I do, feel free to finalize the sale. He'll give you an envelope with the right amount of money, and you give him the keys."

"How will I know if it's the right amount?"

"No sweat. I've sold Grady automobiles in the past, and he's as honest as a preacher."

"Then I'm on my way."

Randolph stepped out of the Cadillac and listened to the roar of the mufflers as the heavy machine sped away.

Rosa Lee headed up the mountain to her destination feeling good that Randy had referred to Grady as *our* customer, not *his* customer. She was also honored that he trusted her to finalize the transaction.

She did exactly as she was told. She located a parking place near the front entrance of Mama's Home Cooking restaurant, got out and marched inside. The place was almost filled; but as luck would have it, the booth they most often occupied was vacant. She made her way to the booth; and within minutes, Irene was placing a menu in front of her.

"Traveling alone, are you?"

"Just for the moment, Randy will be along soon. Say, have you seen a chubby fellow with a mustache in this morning?"

"Oh you mean Grady, Randolph's buddy; no, he hasn't been in today."

Rosa Lee ordered the ham and eggs special and sipped coffee while she waited for Irene to return. She kept an eye on the front entrance so as not to miss seeing Grady, but the next man to enter was anything but short and stocky, and he did not have a mustache. Instead, he was a tall clean-shaven, well-dressed gentleman who carried himself like one with authority. He sat at the bar, just a few feet away from Rosa Lee and ordered a tall glass of orange juice. When Irene returned with his order, he asked if she knew the party who was driving the new Caddy.

Irene nodded, and pointed to Rosa Lee. The gentleman picked up his juice glass and came to her booth. "Mind if I join you?" he asked.

She saw no harm in sharing her space with such a well-mannered gentleman but before she could answer he was seated across from her. "Does the black Cadillac parked near the front door belong to you, ma'am?"

"Oh no, It belongs to Mr. Patrick, I just work for him. He's part owner in an automobile dealership."

"Yes. I've heard of this Mr. Patrick, but I thought his car business was out on the coast. How long have you known him?"

"Not long, two or three months maybe, is that important?"

"Not really, I thought I might be interested in one of his Caddies. What is your position with his company, if you don't mind me asking?"

"I just help Randolph, I mean Mr. Patrick, deliver the cars to their new owners."

"Mr. Patrick sells a lot of cars, does he?"

She was about to elaborate further when she saw the stocky gentleman Randolph had described enter the restaurant. "I guess it's not Mr. Patrick's any longer," she continued. "I'm sure the new owner just walked in; but hang around, I'll be back in a few minutes."

The stranger to whom she had been speaking looked at the new owner then quickly turned in the other direction. "You can count on it," he said as she walked away.

Rosa Lee was so thrilled at the possibility that she might make a sale she hurried to complete the transaction with Randolph's customer.

Her new acquaintance slid close to the wall and sipped his juice until she completed the sale and the customer left the restaurant.

"Gave you cash and you gave him the keys, right" he said when Rosa Lee returned to his table.

"How did you know?"

"Did the fellow tell you his name?"

"No, but he fits the description to a tee, and that's how my boss operates. He says that paying cash ensures them the best price and there is no delivery charge."

He took a business card from his jacket pocket and slid it across the table. "That's Grady Honeycutt, a member of what was one of the largest automobile theft rings in the entire Southeast. He and your boss, Mr. Patrick, spent some time in the crossbar hotel upstate, and I would have thought they would have learned their lesson but I see they are at it again."

Rosa Lee read the card. "Hiram Watts, Special Agent, State of North Carolina."

To be sure she clearly understood, she read it again.

"Are you telling me that Cadillac I just received the cash for was stolen?"

"Now you're getting the picture. There's been a rash of Cadillacs stolen in the past two months, four as a matter of fact. How many have you and Mr. Patrick delivered?"

"How do I know you are really who you say you are?" she asked, her voice barely audible. "What if I just get up and walk out of here?"

"Try it," he said, as he revealed his badge and photo ID, "and I'll have to arrest you before you leave the premises."

"Four," she mumbled.

"Did any of the buyers ask for a title?"

"No, I didn't even think about a title. I suppose I assumed Mr. Patrick would have taken care of any legal papers."

"When he ran his business out on the coast, he sold the stolen automobiles, created counterfeit titles. Now, I see the old boy has wised up. He's running them through a chop shop."

"What's a *chop shop*?" she wanted to know.

"It a place, usually off the beaten path, where the automobiles can be quickly disassembled. The parts are sold at a huge discount."

"You're kidding! Strip the parts off expensive cars such as those brand new Cadillacs?"

The detective shook his head.

Suddenly, Rosa Lee became so frightened, she began to tremble. "What will I do when Randolph comes to pick me up?"

"Nothing. Give him the money and tell him the sale went off without a hitch. I'm going out to report what I have learned to my commander. I'll be back in a moment."

As soon as he was gone, Irene came to her table. "Rosa Lee, what do you know about that fellow Honeycutt?"

Rosa Lee tried her best to play it cool. "Only that he is one of Randolph's associates in the automobile business."

"You mean in the automobile theft business, don't you?"

"What do you mean?"

"Where Honeycutt's been for the last five years, they make automobile license plates, and they also make little rocks out of big ones, I'm told."

"You mean you knew he had been in prison."

"You got it, and your friend Randolph has only been out a short time. I just assumed he'd told you that already. He wasn't incarcerated for nearly as long as a couple of his associates, but I understand that was because he had a smart lawyer who convinced the jury the operation was theirs and not his."

Rosa Lee was anxious to question her further, but the detective reappeared with some questions and suggestions of his own. "I'll make my conversation short and to the point. I'm sure you're expecting Patrick to be taken into custody as soon as he arrives to pick you up, but that will not be the case. We have had him under surveillance for the last couple weeks, long enough to learn that you are guilty only by association. He is simply using you as a patsy as he has done other ladies in the past. I need to know how to contact you whenever it becomes necessary."

Rosa Lee's trembling hand scribbled Jake and Ida Mae's address and phone number on a napkin.

"You must calm down, Mrs. Duncan. If he becomes suspicious, he might cease this operation altogether or move to another location. We don't want that to happen. If we can send him up the river again, I suspect it will be for a long stretch this time."

"Do you think he might do me harm?" She asked.

"Not if you do as you're told. No one is to know what has taken place today. You have my card, and you are to report to me every time he is to make a delivery. And don't worry; if you cooperate with us, I'll see that you are not implicated in any way. And, please don't go out of the state." He gave her a reassuring pat on the hand and left.

"Who was that good-looking gentleman?" Irene asked as soon as he was out of the building.

"Oh, just another one of his customers," she answered as Randolph walked through the front door.

Chapter Thirteen

A SCHEME OF HER OWN

The next few days for Rosa Lee were nerve-wracking to say the least. She had not heard from Randolph or the detective nor had she shared any of the events with her family. She had, however, allowed her admiration for Randolph to turn into pure resentment. She could not believe she had been duped twice in such a short time. She was content to leave the matter of Baxter and the Sutters to Ira and Howard but she would personally make sure Mr. Randolph Patrick paid for getting her involved in his crooked automobile dealings.

Almost a week passed with no word from Randolph, and she was beginning to become somewhat apprehensive so the first time she was left alone, she dialed the number on the card the detective had given her. The phone had barely finished the second ring when she began having second thoughts but it was too late.

"Watts here," a stern voice answered. "Who's calling?"

"This is Granny."

"Who?"

"Oh, I mean Rosa Lee, Rosa Lee Duncan," she stammered.

The detective gave a little chuckle. "You wouldn't be a little nervous now would you, Granny, I mean Rosa Lee, a big time car salesman like you."

"Ah, shut up!" the words were out of her mouth before she had time to think.

This time the detective burst out laughing.

Rosa Lee thought about really giving him a mouthful, but thought it might be to her advantage to allow him to enjoy the moment.

"Another delivery in the making?" he asked.

"No sir," Rosa Lee answered with a voice that was much less abrasive. "I haven't heard a word from Randy, I mean Randolph, since the day I talked with you."

"Then let me fill you in. The day I met you at Mama's Home Cooking I believe your friend was about to get wise to the fact he was being tailed. That's why he sent you to make the delivery by yourself. We could have arrested him that day, but we wanted to give him enough rope to really hang himself, so we backed off. He laid low for about a week, until he felt it was safe to resume his operation I guess, but he is back at it again. A couple new Caddies were stolen from a dealer in High Point last night and we're relatively sure it was your friend Randy," the detective waited for her response. When none came, he continued, "I mean Randolph is responsible. We don't have a clue where he has the vehicles stashed, but we're sure it won't be long until they surface.

"We have reason to believe he is trying to move his operation north into Virginia. If he can find someone he can trust to fence the parts, we're sure that's what he'll do. If he tries to have you drive one of the automobiles across the state line, contact me at once."

"I understand I'm under orders not to leave the state."

"Well, I suppose if it's necessary to help Randy, we can make an exception," he snickered.

Rosa Lee waited a moment before she responded. "Say, what's the penalty for kicking a detective's rear end?"

"Minor. You stay in touch." Rosa Lee could him laugh as the line went dead.

Watts had Patrick figured exactly right. Two days after her conversation with the detective, Patrick came calling. He did not seem as nervous as the last time she saw him, but to her surprise, he was not riding a Cadillac. Instead, he was driving his pickup truck. He pulled up near where she was busy weeding a flower bed and asked if she would like to go for a ride if he came back for her in about an hour.

"Sure enough. Where have you been?"

"Tell you later; see you in an hour."

Rosa Lee was now more anxious than the detective to see Patrick get a one way ticket to the big house. Never in her life had she felt so used or humiliated. Although she trusted Watts, she was determined to see Patrick get his due, even if it meant getting herself in trouble.

She went inside, took a quick shower, and emerged looking her very best. When Randolph returned, she jumped into the pickup and pretended to be excited to spend the day with him.

She endured his small talk for a little while before reminding him he had promised to take her to his place in Bland County. After hesitating for a moment, he agreed it might be a good idea.

"Let's have lunch up on the mountain, and then we'll drive on to your place," she suggested.

"We could do that Rosa Lee; but if you don't mind, there is a fine little diner just out of town I'd like to introduce you to."

Rosa Lee agreed, but she could tell by his demeanor he was in no hurry to return to Mama's Home Cooking. The new establishment was in fact a delight. Although it was small, their waitress was courteous; and the food was delicious. But, when Patrick ordered his third glass of tea, Rosa Lee got the feeling he was simply killing time. Before the end of the day she knew she was correct.

Randolph drove across the state line and made no comment when they passed the restaurant on the mountain. They were little more than a mile into Bland County when he turned onto a narrow road. After four or five miles he stopped near the end of a lane.

"This is where I live, but I have something rather important I have to do later this evening so I won't have time to show you around. I'll drive around the house, and we'll come back again when we have more time, I promise."

As he turned into the lane Rosa Lee determined he must at least be telling her the truth about where he lived because she noticed the faded remains of the name Patrick on the mailbox. And, she was soon to learn what he meant when he said he would drive around his house. As they rounded a curve a beautiful white colonial style home, encircled by a paved driveway, came into view. A Tennessee walking horse was grazing near a bright red barn that stood off to the right. To the left was a long somewhat narrow building with several garage doors.

Randolph drove slowly past the barn while talking of his love for horses. He then rounded the back of the house and was almost past the garage when a middle-aged gentleman wearing oil stained coveralls came out of the building waving his arms. Randolph didn't stop, but he had no choice except to slow down. Before he could speak, the gentleman seemed excited to tell him that those two Caddies that came in the other day was taken care of.

Rosa Lee seemed to take no interest in what the gentleman had said, but Randolph was eager to offer an explanation. "Buf, that's what we call him, his real name is Buford, is our handy man. He cleans our automobiles and makes any necessary adjustments before we deliver them to our customers."

As they drove away, Rose Lee was certain she saw Grady Honeycutt duck back out of sight into the garage. She pretended to be oblivious to what was really taking place, but much of the picture was coming into view. She was certain one of Randolph's associates was stealing the cars in the middle of the night and driving them a short distance where they would be hidden for a short time. When he had given the authorities enough time to give up on finding them, he'd have them brought to his place to be disassembled. She was sure this phase of his operation was also taking place at night, but what she could not figure, was why was he having her deliver them to phony customers in broad daylight.

"That's nice, I'm sure they appreciate it," was all she could muster.

She could not wait to let the detective in on what she had learned. She was sure there was more to this story than she knew, and she was determined to have him fill her in on what was missing.

It was near sundown when Randolph dropped her off on Chestnut Street, and all the family was home which afforded her no chance to call the detective. Any fear she previously may have had was now pure anxiety. She would have liked nothing more than to make her family aware of her involvement in bringing this outlaw to justice, but the embarrassment of having fallen prey to his scheme far outweighed this thought. She fabricated answers to her granddaughter's questions about the events of the day, but she fell asleep with the full assurance her revenge on Mr. Randolph Patrick would be forthcoming.

Up before anyone the following morning, her first act was to place a call to Detective Watts.

"Hello, at this hour, this better be important." The sleepy voice on the other end made her aware she may have called much too early, but it was too late for a second thought.

"Mr. Watts, this is Rosa Lee Duncan." She was about to dive into her findings about Patrick when the detective interrupted.

"Why, Mrs. Duncan, the car saleslady; it's mighty nice of you to call at five o'clock in the morning, but I'm really not in the mood to purchase another vehicle at the moment."

"But I have some important information about Randolph Patrick."

"Tell you what," the detective added, "I was about to begin the first day of vacation in another couple of hours; but since I'm already awake, I might just as well start right now. It will be my first in more than two years so if you don't mind, just make notes about the actions of Mr. Patrick and I'll call you in two weeks. Have a good day."

The phone went dead, and Rosa Lee was about to call him back and tell him what he could do with his vacation and his notes but decided that might not be a good idea. She had no choice but to do as she was told.

Her notekeeping events began to take place the day after the detective left. Randolph arrived early in the morning and seemed excited to tell her about another sale he had made. "The customer wants to take delivery at three, tomorrow afternoon; and I have to be out of town until around six, It will be up to you to drive the car to your favorite eating place, Mama's Home Cooking. The customer will give you the money; and as usual, you'll give him the keys."

Rosa Lee could hardly believe he would think she was such a redneck as to not be aware there was something illegal about these transactions, but she decided she'd play along.

"Not a problem," she assured him and at that moment decided she would do a little detective work of her own. "How will I recognize this customer?" she asked.

"He's tall, he has red hair, and a scar on his chin. I'll pick you up around noon and drive you downtown to where the Caddie is parked."

"I'll be ready."

Her thoughts were to get the money and tell Randolph she was sure his dealings were not on the up and up. She would ask him to double her hundred dollars per deal. That seemed like a reasonable way of having him trust her enough to take her into his dealings. She would learn enough in two weeks to fill an entire notebook for the detective. If things went as she planned, she would teach Mr. Randolph Patrick a lesson he could think about for some time. She could hardly wait for noon to set her plans into action.

Patrick arrived right on time. He acted overjoyed that he was closing so many sales and thrilled that he could depend on Rosa Lee to help make the deliveries.

He drove her to the parking lot where the Caddie was waiting, gave her the keys and said, "I'll see you around six, and we'll have the largest steak on the menu."

We'll have the largest steak in the house, Rosa Lee thought, as she pulled off the lot; but when I tell him what I have in mind, he might have indigestion. Within ten minutes, she was out of town; and an hour later, she was driving up the mountain toward Mama's restaurant. She was so lost in her thoughts she was doing eighty before she knew what was happening.

But, to her surprise there was someone who knew what was happening for suddenly flashing lights appeared in her rear view mirror, and the sound of a screaming siren got her full attention. She was so frightened she almost panicked. She slammed on the brakes so hard all four tires left tread marks as they went scooting off the shoulder of the highway. The officer who was not expecting such action locked the brakes on his cruiser, but he was not quick enough. He plowed right into the back of the new Cadillac.

If clocking the automobile so far above the posted speed limit was not enough to raise his temper, having his patrol car locked to the bumper of the Caddie was enough to do the trick. The officer jumped from the driver's seat and stomped to the side of the Cadillac. "Good afternoon, ma'am; late for lunch, I suppose."

"Oh, no thank you, I've already eaten," she answered, but immediately realized that was not a good answer.

"Don't tell me you were trying to break the land speed record."

"No sir, I am just hurrying to deliver this car to the new owner."

"I hope you won't mind showing me the registration, so I may determine the present owner." Rosa Lee could tell she was pushing his patience to the limit. She was sure she was now going to do something right; but when she opened the door to the glove compartment it was completely empty.

"No registration?"

Rosa Lee simply shook her head.

"Then may I trouble you to show me your driver's license?"

"Uh, I haven't had time to make my permit, but I'm going to right away." Another stupid reply she decided.

When the officer asked for personal identification, she struck out again. She had nothing in her possession to prove who she was.

The officer copied the vehicle identification numbers and asked if she'd mind enjoying the scenery while he radioed his dispatcher. A few moments later he returned with a list of offenses that he asked her to sign. The list included speeding, reckless driving, no registration, and possession of a stolen vehicle. "Hope you don't have plans for dinner, Mrs. ____?"

"Duncan."

"I'm told they serve pretty good food to the prisoners there in Mt. Airy, Mrs. Duncan. Now would you mind having a seat in the back seat of my cruiser?"

She followed the officer back to the police car just as the tow truck arrived. While watching the Cadillac being hooked to the truck, she weighed her options. She was reluctant to give her true identity and admit her involvement in selling stolen automobiles, but she wasn't looking forward to being locked up either.

"Tell him to stop," she told the officer.

"I beg your pardon."

"My name is Rosa Lee Duncan; my son is a sheriff, and this car is stolen."

"I don't know about your first two statements, but the last one I'm sure is correct."

"Really, Ira Duncan is the sheriff up in Russell County."

"Never heard of a Sheriff Duncan."

"Randolph Patrick stole this car, and I delivering it to the person he sold it to."

"Never heard of this Patrick fellow either, and I must warn you anything you say can be held against you."

"You mean I'm under arrest!"

"No ma'am I'm just getting ready to give you a tour of the county. Certainly you're under arrest!"

The tow truck was about to pull away and Rosa Lee realized she was heading nowhere and getting there fast so she played the only trump card she had. "I bet you know Judge Duff."

"Certainly, everyone for miles around knows Judge Sidney Duff. I guess you're going to tell me you're his sister."

"Fiancé." The word ran off her tongue like butter off hot molasses.

"Oh yeah, and I'm going to be the best man; I can't wait to tell Sidney about this one," the officer said in the midst of laughter.

"Call him!" her voice was more like a command than a request.

"You're serious, aren't you?"

"Tell your dispatcher to get the judge, I mean Sidney on the phone. He'll tell you whether or not I'm serious."

"Hold up," the officer called to the truck driver.

"All right Mrs. Duncan, or whoever you are, I'll try to have our dispatcher call Judge Duff only because he and I are friends. Although I seriously doubt it, I might be doing an acquaintance of his a favor. Be forewarned; however, if you are lying to me, that will be another charge added to your already growing list."

Rosa Lee sat on the edge of the seat, biting her nails, as the officer began the call, "Car 1428 to dispatch." After what seemed like a full minute and no answer, he repeated the call. This time the dispatcher responded almost immediately. "Go ahead 1428."

"Good afternoon, Joe, this is Carl. I hope I haven't disturbed your afternoon nap, but would you get Judge Duff on the phone, please?"

"Sorry, Carl, I'm afraid I can't do that."

"Why not, you rascal, are you in the middle of another game of checkers with Sidney?"

"Well, as a matter of a fact, I am."

"Then you'll have to wait while I speak to him."

The dispatcher left the microphone open as he continued to speak. "Judge, car 1428, says he wants to talk to you; but remember it's my move."

"Hey, Carl, what's going on?"

"I have a lady in custody who has nothing to prove who she is but insists you can vouch for her."

"What you got her for?"

"Speeding, reckless driving, no driver's license, driving a stolen vehicle; and I'm about to charge her with causing damage to county property."

"My goodness, man, with charges like that against her why are you calling me? Is she holding a gun on you?"

"No sir, but she is pretty persuasive."

"What's her name, Capone?"

"No sir, she says her name is Duncan, Rosa Lee Duncan."

"Never heard of her."

"Wilcox, tell him my name is Rosa Lee Wilcox."

"Just a minute, Your Honor, she's changed her name again. Maybe it really is Capone but she says it's Wilcox, and she's delivering a stolen car for a Mr. Randolph Patrick."

"Ask her if she knows a fellow by the name of Watts."

The radio went silent for a moment then, "Says she does, but he's on vacation."

"Where this outlaw from?"

Again there was silence on the radio.

"Virginia."

"Then turn her loose, Carl."

"Turn her loose!! Are you serious?"

"Get her phone number, then let her go. Tell her I'll call first thing in the morning.

"Joe, are you sure the judge is okay?"

"He looks just fine to me."

Chapter Fourteen

A Brush with the Law

It was an eventful day for Rosa Lee to say the least. Her involvement with the officer caused her to be a half-hour late getting to the restaurant. Once there, the red- haired gentleman acted as if he wasn't interested in purchasing a damaged vehicle; but when she convinced him her boss would cover the cost of any repairs, he gave her the cash. She was certain his concern for the damage was truly an act, but she had to sound convincing in order to keep them believing she was completely unaware of their scheme.

It wasn't until she watched the red-haired gentleman drive away that the realization of what she'd done hit her. The thought of how close she'd come to being in over her head made her tremble.

"You look like you've seen a ghost," Irene said as she set a cup of coffee in front of her. "Don't tell me you are still involved with Randolph."

Rosa Lee raised the cup, but her hands were shaking so bad coffee splattered all over the table.

"How long have you known him?" Rosa Lee asked.

"All my life; Randy and I grew up together here on the mountain. Comes from a rather well-to-do family too. He has two brothers who have become quite successful. They've owned an automobile dealership for years, but I guess Randolph has told you that already."

"Yes, I believe he told me he was in the car business when we first met."

"He's in the car business all right, but it's usually not very long at a time. He steals a few, sells them for half price. When he feels the law is getting wise to his operation he moves or just lays low for a while."

"How does he keep getting away with it?"

"He involves people like you; then if they get caught, guess who goes up the river. I think you're a nice lady, Rosa Lee; take my advice and cut your ties with Randolph before you wind up in big trouble. Just yesterday, he told me that if he knew someone up in Virginia who would like to purchase some cars real cheap he could make them a real deal. If he's moving his business out of state that could only mean one thing; the authorities are after him again."

"Thanks, Irene, but nobody is going to make a fool of me and get away with it . . . well, almost nobody," she added as the thought of Baxter came to mind.

There were no customers in the restaurant so Irene poured herself a cup of coffee and chatted with Rosa Lee for the better part of an hour. The longer they talked, the more determined Rosa Lee became to make sure Mr. Randolph Patrick was to learn he was not dealing with the simple-minded redneck he assumed her to be.

As their conversation continued, a plan began to formulate in Rosa Lee's head. "Are the two of you real close?" she asked.

"Me, heck no. He's tried more than once to involve me in his shenanigans."

"Then will you help me teach him a lesson?"

"Sure, why not." Rosa Lee was about to reveal her plan, when Irene abruptly interrupted. "Here he comes, we'll talk later." She quickly walked to the other side of the dining room as Randolph came in.

He strolled over to Rosa Lee's table. "Ready for that steak?" he asked. He gave Irene their order, patted Rosa Lee's hand, and told her he was proud of her.

"But I had a little accident; it wasn't real serious so I told the gentleman you would take care of the needed repairs."

"I know."

"You know?"

"I mean, I knew you would be able to handle any minor detail that might arise."

Rosa Lee was sure he knew. His pretense of being out of town was an excuse to distance himself from the area. She was even more determined to show this hotshot a thing or two.

After finishing their meal and driving back to Winston, Randolph raved on about his plans for another big deal. "Do you know some half-wit up where you're from that would like to make some fast bucks? I'm thinking of expanding my sales territory."

When they first met she'd thought he had romantic feelings for her but she now knew she was simply being used. "If my plan materializes, you'll find out which of us has made the biggest deal," she said when he was far enough away she could not be heard.

Now that Randolph was no longer her concern for the day, she turned her thoughts to the call she was to get in the morning. She had no idea how she was going to explain to Sidney how she knew to have the traffic officer get in touch with him, nor how she even knew he was a judge. Being on the opposite side of the law was not a great concern. The last time she saw him, he was being pursued by railroad detectives for illegally transporting moonshine. Anyway, as the day came to a close, she decided he had probably forgotten about her years ago.

* * * * * *

A gentle knock on her bedroom door, and Ida Mae's voice awakened her the following morning. "Granny, you have a phone call. The gentleman said to apologize for calling so early, but that it's really important. "

"What time is it, dear?" Granny asked, sounding as if she were not fully awake.

"Ten o'clock."

"What day is it?"

"Saturday"

"Then tell him to call back later."

Ida Mae started down the stairs to give the gentleman the message when suddenly Rosa Lee's door burst open and she rushed past her.

"I got it, Honey."

Ida Mae was so surprised all she could say was, "I believe you do."

Fifteen minutes later Rosa Lee came into the kitchen where Ida Mae was preparing breakfast. Rosa Lee was bubbling over with excitement. "Guess what, he's not married."

"Wonderful."

"He wants to take me to dinner tonight."

"Great.

"Says we might even go to church tomorrow."

"Nice."

"And he says I shouldn't worry about being in trouble with the law either."

"Now that really is good news. What in the world are you talking about?"

"Don't have time to explain, I have to start getting ready."

"I thought you said this fellow was taking you to dinner."

"That's correct, but he's coming early; five o'clock, I believe he said"

Jake, who had been enjoying his first cup of coffee as he read the morning paper, could stand the suspense no longer. "Who?" He asked.

"Sidney, the judge," Rosa Lee answered as she hurried from the kitchen and headed to the staircase.

"Now isn't that a switch?" he mumbled as he settled back into the morning news.

Ida Mae was as surprised as Jake to hear Granny had finally made contact with her old beau and they were both bewildered about what she meant about being in trouble with the law.

For the next two hours, Rosa Lee ran around like a hungry dog in a butcher shop. She put on a blue dress with all the matching accessories and came downstairs seeking her granddaughter's approval. A short time later, she appeared in a dress of a different color and the ritual would be repeated. After the third change, Jake suggested that since it was rather cool, she just wear all of them. This was after Rosa Lee was out of hearing distance, of course.

"Cool it, Jake; she's just excited." Ida Mae warned.

"How can you tell?" he laughed.

Chapter Fifteen

SECOND TIME AROUND

For at least a week following her first date with the judge, Rosa Lee acted like a ten-year-old on her first trip to the zoo. She was up at the crack of dawn, chattering about what she and Sidney were going to do that day, if anyone else was up early enough to listen. Some mornings she would prepare a picnic lunch for another trip somewhere out of the city, and she almost never got back home until late at night. When the girls would ask about their events of the day, her answer was always the same, "I'm just too tired to talk about it now; I'll tell you later."

By the week's end, Ida Mae and Mary Sue could stand the suspense no longer. On Friday evening, they seated themselves under the magnolia tree near the curb and waited for their grandmother and Sidney to arrive. They talked of their mistrust about their granny's friend, the hotshot salesman, Randolph Patrick, and her renewed excitement in getting reacquainted with her old fiancé.

Jake, on the other hand, was not at all interested in Rosa Lee's love life. In fact he had chosen to spend the weekend down in Charlotte watching his brother, J.D. burn some rubber on the racetrack.

J.D was beginning to win a few races and earning his own fan club around the racing circuit. More and more drivers were beginning to respect his ability to maneuver the Green Dragon around the track. He was at last earning more than enough money at his job and on the track to keep his car in top running condition and his calls to Mary Sue were becoming more frequent.

"I'm sure it won't be long until she sends one of them packing; and when she does, I sure hope it's Patrick." Ida Mae commented.

"Speak of the devil, Sis," Mary Sue added, as a snow-white Cadillac stopped just a few feet from where they were seated.

"Afternoon ladies. Is Ms. Rosa Lee at home? I thought she and I might go for a drive, and I could tell her how wonderful sales have been this week."

Mary Sue wanted to tell him that if he would wait around for a while, a Circuit Court Judge would be stopping by, and he might sell him a new one if the price was right; instead, she bit her tongue. "No sir, she's taking care of some business and won't be back until very late."

"Will you please tell her I'll be by early Monday morning, because we'll need to deliver one of these beauties down to High Point?"

Mary Sue thought about saying if he had two to deliver, the judge would probably like to drive one of them; however she promised to relay his message.

The uppity Mr. Patrick had barely gotten out of sight when Granny and the judge arrived. The judge's car had barely come to a stop when both ladies were there to greet them. Mary Sue was the first to speak. "Hope the two of you don't have plans for dinner Sunday evening because we're having T-bones right off the grill, and Jake's doing the cooking. If that's okay with you, Your Honor."

Rosa Lee nodded her approval.

"We'd be delighted, but it's no longer Your Honor. In another month I'll no longer be on the bench, even as a substitute, so please call me Sidney. I trust you have been behaving since our last meeting, young lady." The comment was directed at Mary Sue.

"She's doing great with her studies, but she hits the bars almost every weekend," Ida Mae was quick to inform him.

"So I've heard. Rosa Lee tells me you can sing like a humming bird, and you're in demand all over the city. I can't wait to be in the audience during one of your performances."

"Thanks, Your Honor, I mean Sidney; but you can't believe everything you hear."

"How's your partner in crime, Mr. Hurd? Is he staying out of trouble or is he hitting the bars also?"

Quick witted, Ida Mae was first to answer again, "He's speeding almost every time he gets behind the wheel; and as of late, he's been hard to catch."

"Your grandmother tells me he's becoming one of the favorites when he's on the track."

"What else have you been telling the judge?" Ida Mae asked.

"Very little," Sidney answered. "Each time I try to inquire about her family, she keeps wanting to know what I've been doing for the last forty years."

"That's right" Rosa Lee admitted, "and I've learned a lot about some very high-profile cases. Would you believe Sidney has a large storage building filled with transcripts of every case he's presided over since he's been on the bench?"

"Not all the space is filled with transcripts. I left room for a few other items" Sidney added. "May I see you tomorrow, Rosie?"

"You bet," she said as her face turned the color of a newly blossoming pink rose.

The two girls went back inside while the couple said their good-byes. In a short while, Rosa Lee came through the front door and headed upstairs for her bath and bed.

The mischievous granddaughters waited until she reached the top landing and then in perfect harmony, "Good night, Rosie."

"And by the way Mr. Patrick said to tell you he'd pick you up early Monday morning. He said something about a delivery to High Point."

"Oh, he did, did he?" was their granny's last comment before the bedroom door closed behind her.

Rosa Lee was in bed right away but sleep did not come at once. She lay awake for hours trying to figure out how to prove to Mr. Randolph Patrick she was not the fool he assumed her to be. She'd had to tell Sidney very little about being drawn into Patrick's illegal automobile dealings. The judge knew more about how he operated than she did. He was the one who had sent him and his cronies up the river the first time.

I'd heard he was out of prison, and was looking for unsuspecting drivers to help him get rid of his hot merchandise as quickly as possible Sidney had told her. I'd also heard he moved his operation back to this area and that Detective Watts was closing in on him. When I overheard the deputy give the name Rosa Lee Wilcox to the dispatcher I became so excited I almost forgot whose move it was.

Rosa Lee was embarrassed to have been so gullible as to become involved in Randolph's scheme. She was willing to aid the police in shutting down his entire business but she had a personal score to settle. It was nearly two in the morning before she had all the details worked out. All she needed was a little help from Irene; and if her plan worked, she'd have enough bait to set a trap that would end Patrick's schemes forever. She'd take Irene up to her home in Virginia and have her meet the Sutters, quite by accident of course. After two or three visits Irene would promise them a way to make some quick cash if they could come up with a few hundred dollars up-front to invest. Rosa Lee was sure they were so poor they could barely pay attention. Unless she missed her guess, they would go straight to their landlord, William Baxter. If she were correct, Baxter would not hesitate to make some big bucks, legal or not.

She knew she would have to trust Irene and only the two of them could know. She couldn't even tell Sidney because if her plan worked, and she knew it would, it might be construed as entrapment. When she had all the details worked out to her satisfaction she fell into a deep sleep. She was so proud of her plans, she became so relaxed she slept the following day until way past noon. When she did put on her robe and start creeping slowly down the stairs, Mary Sue yelled to Ida Mae, "Cancel the call for the ambulance, Sis; she really was just sleeping."

"Don't you girls ever have a serious thought?" she asked as she made her way into the living room.

"Sure do. Mom called earlier today, and we have some really wonderful news. Daddy is improving much faster than any of us expected, and the doctor says he can go back to work whenever he feels he's able."

"That is wonderful news, and he'll be back on duty tomorrow, if I know your daddy. Any other calls, for me I mean?"

"Oh yes," Mary Sue was quick to answer, "Sidney called four times, but we told him you were so ill you had taken to your bed, and he probably shouldn't call again."

Rosa Lee was about to make some comment that would have been just as ridiculous, but the phone began ringing before she could speak.

"Hello. It sure is, and I've made a remarkable recovery. Oh no, I'm fine; I'll explain later. I'm just carrying on with my fun-loving granddaughters. Just a moment. Sidney wants to know if it would be okay if he brings someone with him to the cookout Sunday evening."

"Mary Sue said it would be okay if he's young, single, rich and good looking."

"Tell her she'll just have to wait and see when we get there."

"I'll tell her, and I'll see you this evening".

"What a treat," Ida Mae sang out. "You'll have all afternoon to tell us what you've learned about Sidney. We haven't seen you more than half-hour at a time since you met him you know. Jake won't be home until tomorrow morning, and there's no one here but us girls so tell us all about your new heart throb."

"And don't leave out any of the romantic parts," Mary Sue added.

"I hardly know where to begin, young'uns; but I will say Sidney has had a very interesting life. I'll tell you the story of his life just as he told it to me."

"Start from the time he jumped off the porch and left you up in the mountains forty odd years ago," Ida Mae suggested.

"Well, it's like this," Rosa Lee began. "The day Sidney made his narrow escape he headed straight for the railroad and caught the first night train heading for West Virginia. He did not travel as a passenger as he customarily did; he became a hobo. And he didn't go back to the same counties where he and our daddys worked for fear he'd be caught by the railroad detectives. Instead, he traveled further north almost into Maryland. He got a job in a lumber camp at a sawmill where he worked as a dust doodler. The job required shoveling sawdust that fell underneath the huge blade into a wheel barrow then rolling it to the end of the sawdust pile, dumping it over the edge and then going back for another load. It was back-breaking labor but he felt it was probably the last place the railroad detectives would look for him.

"He hid out at the logging camp for the first six months with no contact with the outside world. After that time, he got brave enough to begin writing letters home, with a fictitious name as the return address. In his very first letter, he asked his mom to have me wait for him. He asked me to remember his promise that he would come for me as soon as he earned the money to purchase his Model T; but by that time it was too late; I'd already married your grandfather. He admitted he was heart broken, but he never mentioned me in any of his letters again. Years later, he met and married a lady from here in North Carolina. A short decade later, she died of cancer. He admits he's dated on several occasions, sometimes ladies who were much younger, but never considered getting married again."

For the first time Ida Mae interrupted her grandmother's story. "Did they have children?" she asked.

"None." Rosa Lee stated then continued with her account of what happened to Sidney during the years they were out of touch.

"It was while working at the mill he met and become friends with Burley Whitmore. Burley, Sidney learned weeks later, was not the young fellow's name, but a nickname he earned because of his size. He was really somewhat of a muscular young gentleman, according to Sidney; about six feet five, and tipped the scales near two hundred fifty pounds. His job as off-bearer required stacking the heavy lumber onto the proper stack, a job which required strong muscles. Burley had no trouble performing his duties.

"Burley, not only possessed strong muscle, he also had a brilliant mind. He, like Sidney, had ambitions of making his mark in society some day. He wanted desperately to become a trial lawyer, one who defended clients in high profile cases. The dream of becoming an attorney suited Sidney to a tee. He had someone with whom he could share his goals. They talked of little else. Each evening while the other workers gathered after the evening meal to tell jokes and have a few drinks, Burley and Sidney buried themselves in law books. They would study various cases in which clients were severely punished or sometimes acquitted and discuss what they, as trial lawyers, would have done differently.

"Sidney eventually moved from a bunkhouse he shared with a dozen other workers to a smaller one where Burley lived. Their evenings were spent studying the procedures of practicing law on both civil and criminal levels. They were so intent on fulfilling their goals that when there was some rather minor dispute among the workers, someone would jokingly recommend the law firm of Duff and Whitmore. Although it was all done in fun, the idea of being partners in law was appealing to both the young men.

"Sidney worked at various jobs in and around the logging camps for the better part of three years. On rare occasions, he would leave the camp and go into the nearest town with some of the other workers. These were usually small settlements where coal miners and loggers would go to relax after a hard week's labor. Many of the small towns were filled with bars, gambling houses, and other places where money could get away in the wink of an eye. Sidney admits he was no saint; but like Burley he seldom visited these night spots. They worked overtime hours, holidays, and weekends saving almost every dollar in hopes of one day enrolling into law school.

"Sidney stayed close to camp for fear that if he did otherwise he might still be sought after by the railroad detectives. Burley, Sidney learned months after they met, had no place to go for he was an orphan.

"The summers were long and the work was hard; but by staying busy, time seemed to pass quickly. The winters in the counties of Northern West Virginia could be harsh. Sometimes it would snow for days, and it would be too dangerous to bring the logs down from the deep hollows or high ridges which meant the mills would come to a halt.

"This was the case during the beginning of the fourth winter that Sidney worked at the mills. There had been a furious storm causing the mills to be idle for days. The workers had been shut in so long the least disagreement would sometimes escalate into a major argument. For Sidney and Burley, the problem was sheer boredom. Early one morning during one of these depressed times, the two want-to-be attorneys set out for parts further South. They packed all their worldly goods in one faded, mud-colored brown grip that belonged to Burley and left the logging camp for their last time. They began their journey with no destination in mind and with no means of getting there.

"To Sidney, a mode of transportation was not a problem. He'd ridden the rails many times before, and he was sure he could do it again. They walked until mid-afternoon before reaching the nearest section of the railroad. They hovered among the thick underbrush for another hour to shield themselves from the bitter cold wind. They didn't have the foggiest idea what time the next locomotive would pass or in what direction it would be traveling; but one thing for certain, they intended to be on it. While waiting for the train, Sidney tried to teach Burley the art of becoming a hobo. Burley learned the lesson well. When the sound of an approaching southbound broke the silence of the cold winter day, the couple hovered lower into the thick undergrowth so as not to be seen by the engineer. As soon as Sidney deemed it was safe, they made their move. They could not have been luckier, for several boxcars with open doors were moving rather slowly toward them.

"Sidney started running along side the train with Burley right on his heels. When their gate was almost equal to the speed of the train, Sidney threw their suitcase inside one of the cars and yelled, 'Grab hold and jump.' He landed inside the boxcar, and the overgrown Burley landed smack on top of him.

"'Where to now Captain?' Burley asked when he'd rolled himself off Sidney and onto a large pile of golden colored fresh smelling straw.

"'Anywhere where we can go barefoot in winter,' Sidney suggested.

"That's exactly what they did; they closed the doors on the boxcar snuggled into the bed of straw and rode through the night. The sound of the huge steel wheels grinding against the rails was all that was necessary to put the two tired travelers to sleep.

"The clatter of the couplings being tightened as the train slowed brought both men into an upright position. As the train came to a stop, Sidney opened the door of the boxcar only a few inches but enough to tell they were surrounded by street lights. Burley rubbed his eyes, pulled enough straw from his hair to make a hen's nest and asked where they were. Sidney had to admit he had no idea but confessed it was exactly where he wanted to be because he could smell fresh bacon being fried somewhere nearby.

"As it turned out, Sidney told me they were in the South side of Richmond, Virginia.

"When Sidney mentioned food nothing else mattered for the moment. Burley grabbed the suitcase and was off the train in an instant.

"Their stay in Richmond was brief, only long enough to fill their empty bellies and catch the next train heading south. The final stop on their journey was in the central part of North Carolina. They secured lodging in a boarding house, found employment in a furniture factory and were soon enrolled in a law school.

"Sidney had to confess he had not finished his senior year in high school but scored so high on his entrance exam he was permitted to enroll, provided he maintain passing scores throughout the first semester.

"To both Sidney and Burley, passing the first semester was a piece of cake. They'd studied criminal cases and legal procedures in as many law library books as was available in the small towns near the logging camps where they had worked.

"Working at the furniture factory was extremely hard but, fortunately for the two law students, many weeks the workdays were short. If orders for furniture were few, they might only work for a few hours each week. If, on the other hand, orders increased, their hours of work would increase. This suited both Sidney and Burley because all they required was enough cash for food and boarding house rent. Money for entertainment was out of the question. Every waking hour not required at the factory was spent on their studies. At the end of three years, they had finished law school and passed the bar exam.

"Burley graduated first in his class and was offered a junior partnership in a law firm somewhere near Baltimore. They two said farewell a week after graduation and had no contact with each other until almost six months ago. They now talk on the telephone at least once a week and are planning to get together again real soon.

"Sidney admits he was not as lucky as his old roommate. He stayed on at the furniture factory for almost a full year and continued living in the boarding house. With Burley gone, his rent doubled, but work at the factory picked up, and he was able to do a small amount of legal work for some of his fellow workers: deeds, wills, title searches and the like. There were an ample number of law offices in the area, but none who were willing to take another attorney. So, Sidney did the only other thing he knew to do, he rented a small one room office tucked half-way back in an alley and hung up his shingle.

"It was nearing the end of the first year after Burley had left that Sidney got his first real case. A young man, who we'll say lived among the less fortunate, was accused of murdering another fellow from the elite side of town. As it were, the young man who was murdered was the son of an attorney. The evidence against the defendant appeared to be pretty much cut-and-dried so no other lawyer in the city would take the case. But Sidney, who believed the young man's story, agreed to defend him, for a very modest fee, of course.

"The case dragged on for weeks. Sidney spent all that he had charged his client and most of his own savings following leads that pointed to others who might have had reason to commit the crime.

"It was nearing the end of the trial, and it seemed Sidney had exhausted all avenues of defense when the prosecutor made the mistake of putting the deceased's girlfriend on the stand. During cross examination Sidney got her so bewildered she admitted being present when her current lover killed her former boyfriend in the midst of a jealous rage.

"Within thirty days of successfully defending his client Sidney had more business than he could handle. Needless to say, he moved his office onto Main Street where he remained until being appointed judge some twenty years later.

"About the same time he moved his office, a coffee shop opened directly across the street, and Sidney became a regular customer. He stopped every morning for coffee and a quick bite to eat, if his heavy schedule permitted. A few weeks after the establishment opened, the owner hired a beautiful new waitress. It was then Sidney managed to make time for a lengthy early morning meal and a bit of conversation even if something at his office had to be moved a little further into the day. He soon found himself crowding lunch into his busy schedule; and before the end of the year, he and the young waitress were married.

"Sidney bought a place outside of town, and his new bride gave up her job at the coffee shop to become his receptionist at the law office. She planned to work until they started a family, but that was not to be. For shortly after their marriage the young bride's health begin to fail. She was diagnosed with cancer. In spite of being treated for several years by the very best physicians in the Carolinas it was determined there was no known cure. Shortly after their tenth anniversary, she was laid to rest; and Sidney never remarried.

"He is now retired and spends his time on his small secluded two acre estate about ten miles outside Mt. Airy. He spends many hours reviewing the transcripts of some of the most high profile cases he's tried. As a judge, he admits there have been times when smart lawyers have persuaded jurors to allow defendants he believed to be guilty to go free. The cases that stand out most in his memory are those involving defendants who might have been innocent, but were found guilty. Although the law required him to do so, sentencing those defendants tore at the deepest fibers of his inner being. That, Sidney admits, is why he has kept transcript copies of every case he defended or heard while on the bench.

"When I asked what he would most like to do now that he was retired, he quickly replied, 'Move back to the mountains in Virginia where I spent my childhood.'

The girls listened intently as their grandmother recalled her old boyfriend's past as it was told to her. They were so engrossed in her story neither wanted it to end but the telephone rang.

Chapter Sixteen

A MESSAGE FROM HOME

Rosa Lee, the closest to the telephone, answered. "Hello, yeah this is she," the conversation began. The girls began whispering about Sidney so as not to disturb their grandmother The longer the phone conversation went on the more excited their grandmother became and the whispering stopped. Ida Mae and Mary Sue were suddenly all ears.

"You don't say, tell me more, I mean exactly how it happened. Glory Bee, that's the most exciting news since I heard the war ended."

The more excited Rosa Lee became the more anxious the girls were to find out what it was that had her so worked up.

The phone call lasted for a full thirty minutes, longer than any of them had ever talked before. Rosa Lee barely had time to hang up the phone when Mary Sue had her by the arm almost dragging her to the sofa. "Tell us what happened."

Rosa Lee gave a long sigh and allowed herself to be seated, "I think I need a cup of coffee," she mumbled.

"Aren't you going to tell us about the phone call first?" Mary Sue questioned.

"You get me a cup of coffee please, while I sort out exactly what it was that I heard."

Not one but both ladies rushed to the kitchen to fetch their grandmother her much needed cup of coffee. Ten minutes later they were back to learn what the phone conversation was all about.

"I hardly know where to start," Rosa Lee stated and then hesitated to take a long sip from the coffee cup. "You're not going to believe this," she said and took another drink.

Mary Sue could stand the suspense no longer. She took the cup from her grandmother and placed it on the table at the end of the sofa. "Please tell us," she pleaded.

"That was your mother on the line, and she was giving me a rundown on your father's first full shift of work. Last evening's shift began rather uneventful for a Friday night and remained so until shortly after midnight. Howard, Deputy Barton that is, had just marked on duty when your father called and insisted he was going to accompany him. Howard tried to talk him out of returning to work so soon; but your father, being the Sheriff, had the final word.

"It was, as your mother tells me, a rather quiet evening Rather routine as she put it, with only a couple of the local boys who had a few too many bottles of losers cool-aid needing a safe place to sleep for the night. It was after Howard and your father had the young fellows safely locked up in the crossbar hotel and heading back on patrol that the most interesting occurrence of the night started to unfold.

"They were only a mile or so out of town when they began following an older model automobile. After tailing the car for a ways, they could not help but notice it weaving from one side of the highway to the other. They decided to stop the vehicle to see if the operator might be sick, sleepy, or perhaps had too much to drink.

"Howard turned on the emergency lights but the driver ignored the lights, so Howard pulled close to the rear bumper and gave a loud blast on the siren. All of a sudden the brake lights glared, and the car came to a screeching halt without even leaving

Granny's Justice

the pavement. Deputy Barton approached the car on the driver's side; and Ira, on the other. Your father remained silent as Howard gently knocked on the side glass with his flashlight.

"When the young lady who was driving lowered her window a thick cloud of cigarette smoke mixed with the smell of alcohol led him to believe she was most likely not feeling any pain. She identified herself as Louise Wimpler, and she lived near Bristol, Tennessee.

"Howard could see there was a gentleman who appeared to be asleep in the passenger seat and asked who he was and if he had a problem. After several feeble attempts, she told him the guy was her boy friend and that she was lost.

"When he asked where it was she was trying to find, she told him she was looking for the sheriff's house. She said she was helping her boyfriend deliver a "bum" to the sheriff, but he had passed out and she had forgotten where it was the sheriff lived.

"Howard asked where the bum was, and she told him in the back of the car. Howard, thinking maybe another fellow had passed out and they were so intoxicated they'd put him in the trunk, asked if she minded if he checked to see if he was okay. When she told him the "bum" was not a person but a device her boyfriend was planning to use to do away with the sheriff, a routine traffic stop became a lot more serious. It was no secret the lady was stoned out of her gourd and that the "bum" she was talking about was in fact a bomb.

"Howard quickly jerked open the car door and ordered the young lady to step outside the vehicle. He told her she was under arrest and placed her in cuffs. Mary Ellen said that by this time they'd learned her boy friend was none other than Baxter himself. Ira left him lying in the front seat mumbling to himself and joined Howard at the rear of the car.

"When Howard popped open the trunk lid and lit up the rear compartment, both officers looked at each other in disbelief. Lying in plain view were some license plates, one of which was a

Tennessee issue which bore the lettering TKO-123. Also partially hidden under a burlap sack was a short galvanized pipe attached to an alarm clock by some small pieces of wire.

"When the lady asked if she was in trouble, Ira threw so much scare into her she began to rattle on like a parrot being threatened to be served for Thanksgiving dinner. She admitted her real name was Lola Sutter, the only daughter of the family living on Baxter's farm. She further admitted she had become acquainted with Baxter a few months before he was ousted as sheriff.

"Your mother tells me the charges against him began with drunk in public, possession of stolen license plates, attempted murder of a police officer and the list grew from there."

The girls listened to every word as their grandmother told about the phone call.

"What will happen if Baxter is convicted?" Mary Sue questioned.

"Let's just say by the time he gets out of prison, he probably won't be interested in the likes of Miss Lola Sutter."

Chapter Seventeen

THE TRAP

The news from home left Rosa Lee feeling as if the weight of the world had been lifted from her shoulders. She'd no longer spend sleepless nights worrying about what Baxter might do; he had enough of his own worries to keep him busy for a long while. Nor was she deeply concerned about her son's ability to handle other offenders who might get into trouble. After all, Ira knew most of the families living in the county; and with one or two exceptions, they were generally law abiding citizens.

With Baxter at least temporarily out of the picture she could spend time figuring out how to bait the trap that would send Mr. Randolph Patrick up the river. She wasn't about to waste time dwelling on the likes of Patrick at the moment because it would soon be time for her outing with the judge.

Rosa Lee enjoyed every moment with Sidney, and she had no doubt the feeling was mutual. She wasn't sure if he was being so nice just for old times sake or if he still had feelings for her. He'd not mentioned their getting back together, and she could not help remembering the young lady he was with at the restaurant a few weeks earlier. Each time they were together, she wanted to ask about her; but at the last moment, she lost her nerve. He had not known she was even at the same restaurant; and if she told him, it might look as if she were spying. If he did have romantic feelings for the young lady, she was sure she would find out soon enough.

"Better not keep the judge waiting much longer, or he might find you in contempt," Mary Sue called to her granny as Sidney pulled up in front of their house.

Mary Sue joined her older sister who was already enjoying a cool glass of lemonade and the last warm rays of a Carolina setting sun. They watched as Sidney got out of his car with a bouquet of roses in one hand and a box of chocolates in the other. He was dressed in a light blue polo shirt, a pair of dark blue trousers and patent leather shoes that was so brightly polished one could have used them for a mirror. The sunrays danced on his silver hair as he walked toward the front porch in a manner which would lead one to believe he was on a mission.

"Evening ladies, do I have permission to take your grandmother out for the evening?"

"If either of them say no, they will be grounded for a month," Rosa Lee said as she stepped onto the porch. She was wearing a low-cut knee length dress that matched the judge's shirt so well it could have been made from the same piece of cloth.

"Gifts for the loveliest lady in all of Winston," Sidney said, handing Rosa Lee the flowers and candy.

Rosa Lee stood for what seemed a full minute just staring at the candy and roses. At last she turned to Ida Mae as a tear begin to form in the corner of her eye. Sensing her feelings of emotion Ida Mae saved her the effort of trying to speak. "I'll put these in water and hide the chocolates from Mary Sue," she told her grandmother. They would probably never know but both the girls wondered if this was the first time any man had treated her with such great admiration.

"Won't you please come in, Sidney?" Ida Mae added.

"Another time. I have dinner reservations, and I wouldn't want to keep my other guest waiting."

Suddenly, Rosa Lee's expression of admiration turned to one of bewilderment. Was what she hoped was going to be an enjoyable evening alone with Sidney going to be a meeting with some attorney, or even worse, a business meeting of sort?

"I'll have this lovely lady home before midnight," the judge said as he escorted Rosa Lee to his car.

During the twenty-minute drive downtown, Sidney talked of how wonderful it was to be spending another evening with her. Rosa Lee, on the other hand, spoke very little. She was still trying to understand why her date was having someone else along without her knowledge or approval.

The identity of the mystery guest was soon unraveled. Sidney pulled in front of the same restaurant where she had first seen him after more than forty years. The valet took their automobile as they entered the establishment. A waiter greeted the well-known guest and told him his table was waiting and that his guest had already arrived.

The judge gently took Rosa Lee by the arm and followed the waiter across the dimly lit dining room floor. As they neared the booth, Rosa Lee's body became so rigid she almost froze. Even in candle light she was able to recognize Sidney's mystery guest. It was the very same young lady he had dined with the evening she was there with the Wallaces. A rage of jealously shot through her like a bolt of lightning. How dare him bring her out for the evening only to meet a former date.

Secretly, she vowed not to make a scene; but inwardly, she decided that before this night was over, she would feed the judge a line that would surely give him grounds to hold her in contempt.

Sidney pushed, or maybe dragged her the last couple steps toward their booth. "Rosa Lee Duncan I would like you to meet my niece, Miss Haley Barber."

Rosa Lee took a deep breath, and her body became so limp Sidney was barely able to get her seated. "I'm so, so, so, glad,— Hello," was all she could muster. She was so bewildered she didn't know whether to hit him or hug him; but by the end of the evening, she decided the latter would be most appropriate.

Haley, she learned was the daughter of the late Mrs. Duff's sister. Her father was killed in a hunting accident when Haley was only six years old: and by her own choosing, Sidney had taken his place. Having no children of his own, this arrangement suited Sidney just fine.

Haley's mother worked in a furniture factory; but at times, her hours were reduced or eliminated completely. Mrs. Barber was much too proud to ask for help. However during those times of depression, Sidney was always there. Although not officially he adopted Haley. He'd subsidized her college tuition and was instrumental in getting her into one of the finest law schools. One of the most thrilling days in his career was having to disqualify himself as judge because she was representing one of the defendants.

After dinner, Haley insisted they follow her to her apartment for coffee and dessert. Rosa Lee was so relieved at finding out who she really was she would have followed her to the moon. The moment they entered Haley's apartment she could tell just how much she loved and admired her Uncle Sidney. Pictures of her and Sidney were all over the place: at the skating rink, the bowling alley, on the softball field, just to name a few.

Rosa Lee listened to the young lady tell of the wonderful times she and Sidney had had together. How he'd taken her under his wing after the tragic death of her father. How when her mother was out of work and the bills kept coming, there would be an envelope in the mail that contained nothing but cash. There was never a return address, but they both knew who had sent it.

Rose Lee listened to the stories Haley told and answered the many questions asked of her. To her surprise, Haley knew things about her she herself had forgotten nearly half-century ago. Sidney had told Haley that their families had been neighbors up in the hills of Virginia. How he had walked her to school and tried desperately to flirt with her, but to no avail. He also confessed that after he had at last won her affections, his desire to own a Model-T before they were married drove him to do things that was somewhat outside the law.

"He never did tell me what the dreadful crime was that caused him to lose you, but he did promise that someday he might."

From where Rosa Lee sat, the wall clock in the hallway was clearly visible. She watched as the hands crept toward the midnight hour, but she did not want to leave. It became clear that Sidney's affections for his niece were well deserved. By the time they said good night, the beautiful young lady she once felt was her rival seemed more like one of the family. As Haley showed them to the door, she gave each of them a warm embrace and told Rosa Lee she'd see her again at the cookout.

"Is Haley your surprise guest tomorrow afternoon?" Rosa Lee asked.

"She sure is. Isn't Mary Sue going to be surprised?"

On their way home, Rosa Lee learned of Sidney's love of the mountains and his desire to spend his sunset years where he'd spent his childhood.

"Do you ever go back just to visit?" she asked.

"Not very often. I knew the railroad detectives had a warrant so I didn't go back for over six months. I figured they'd decided I had probably left the area for good and placed the warrant in the dead file."

"Why did you not let me know you were back?"

"I wanted to; you were the only reason I took a chance on coming back, but when I learned you were married I decided I'd never go back again. I stayed away for a few years; but when I married, I did make annual visits to see my parents in Grundy."

Rosa Lee slid closer to Sidney just as they turned onto Chestnut street. She took his hand as the car came to a stop. In a voice that was barely more than a whisper, "Sidney, let's go back to the mountains."

"You mean the two of us? Go back together?"

"Why not? We can leave tomorrow."

"We're going to a cookout tomorrow, remember?"

"Then first thing Tuesday morning."

"Tuesday?" he questioned. "Why not Monday?"

"Oh, I already have a date for Monday," she teased.

Sidney thought for a long moment, then the smile Rosa Lee remembered from long ago begin to appear. "Tuesday morning it is."

Rosa Lee was not about to tell Sidney her plans to help Randolph deliver one of his stolen automobiles Monday, nor of her plans to put an end to his scheme.

Chapter Eighteen

JUDICIAL CONFESSIONS

The cookout was truly a blast; and as predicted, Mary Sue most certainly did get a surprise. Sidney's guest was not the rich, good-looking young man she had joked about, but the beautiful Haley Barber. Sidney and his niece, Haley, were the first to arrive. Next came Jake, followed by his brother, J.D., who was driving his rust-colored pickup and towing his race car trailer. J.D. parked near the end of the street and headed straight to the front porch where Mary Sue was sitting. He bounced up in front of her, gave her a kiss on the forehead and asked if she'd missed him.

"Have you been gone?" she teased.

Ida Mae came from inside followed by Sidney and Haley. "Allow me to introduce our guests, and then Jake can fire up the grill. You are chef for the day," she reminded him.

The moment Haley stepped into view ideas began running through J.D.'s head faster than the rpm's in the Green Dragon's engine heading toward the checkered flag. He'd tried for months, with little success, to develop a closer relationship with Mary Sue. He was not about to let an opportunity to make her jealous pass. He pretended to direct all his interest on this new acquaintance.

"Do you enjoy racing?" he asked.

"I don't really know, but I'm sure I would if I knew some of the drivers. Is that what you do for a living?"

"Just part time, on weekends you know, so maybe you could come see me race one day."

Mary Sue pretended to be disinterested in what was being said; but as it became more evident he had little to say to anyone else, she begin to develop a slight tinge of jealousy.

"Are you in school, college I mean?" he asked.

"Oh no. Thanks to Uncle Sidney I'm a practicing defense attorney."

"Wonderful, will you take my case?"

"That depends, sir. What are the charges?"

"Uh, beating up an old lady."

"When and where did this take place?"

"Tomorrow if you will take the case."

Mary Sue turned her head and smiled. She did not want him to know she was amused at his line of bull; but at the first opportunity, she gave him a stare that sent little arrows aimed straight at his heart.

"How long have you known Uncle Sidney?" Haley asked.

"Oh, he met him a few months ago, in the court house as a matter of fact," Mary Sue volunteered.

"Had some legal business to take care of, did you, J.D?"

"You might say that; but your uncle told him exactly what to do," Mary Sue added before J.D. could answer.

"He's good at that," Haley bragged. "I hope you're going to take Uncle Sidney's advice."

J. D. opened his mouth to speak; but again, Mary Sue beat him to the draw. "He'd better! If he tries anything like that again your uncle promised to lock him up."

"You don't mean . . . "

"Yes, he does" Mary Sue interjected one last comment before joining her sister and brother-in-law at the grill.

Granny's Justice

The remainder of the evening went along without incident. Jake and Ida Mae were the perfect host and hostess. The food was delicious, and the early fall setting could not have been more beautiful. The bright orange, fading green, and fiery red leaves painted on a canvas of a clear blue sky was nothing less than nature's way of displaying her magnificent beauty. The squawk of an occasional flock of wild geese en route to the warm waters of the South made it evident winter was knocking at the door.

Sidney and Rosa Lee sat in the porch swing telling of their youth, growing up in the mountains of Virginia. As they talked of their early courtship and of their plans to see the world in Sidney's Model-T, the girls pulled their chairs up closer and hung onto every word. It was when the judge began reminiscing about pulling logs from the ridges and dark hollows in the hills of West Virginia that he captured Jake and J.D.'s attention. To both the boys, Sidney's experiences as a young man were not unlike their own. Even his encounters with the law was familiar. As Sidney told how he moved from one logging camp to another for fear the railroad detectives might learn of his whereabouts, the pale expression which appeared on Haley's face was almost frightful.

"What on earth were you doing, Uncle Sidney?" she asked.

"Transporting moonshine dear," Rosa Lee said without hesitation.

The rosy red cheeks that had a moment earlier turned pale at learning her uncle, the judge, was wanted were now the color of chalk. She had almost reached the point of feeling as if she might pass out.

J.D, on the other hand, was totally surprised and amused. Suddenly, he was aware of why he and Mary Sue had received only a slight reprimand when they were caught transporting shine. After all, how could he hand down a harsh sentence when it was nothing more than he had done.

In a short while Haley managed to regain her composure. She and the other young folks listened to stories about Rosa Lee and Sidney until almost dusk. Some of the incidents they shared about their growing up years, especially their hardships, left their audience in awe. What they didn't tell them was they were planning a trip back to the mountains.

Just as the first golden arch of the rising moon appeared on the horizon, Sidney rose to his feet. "Time I was getting this young lady home, I understand she is due in court in the morning."

Rosa Lee walked with the two of them to the curb. Sidney waited until his niece was inside the car and then whispered, "I'll pick you up at ten; we'll go back home and pretend we are young once again."

"I can hardly wait," she answered as he turned to go, then remembering her appointment with Randolph reached out to him. "Could we wait just one more day, I'll need to pack, we'll be gone for a few days. Right?"

"Marvelous."

Rosa Lee squeezed his aging wrinkled hand and a touch of nostalgia gripped her inner being. For the first time in her life, she allowed herself to face the realization that she too was in the dawn of her sunset years.

Chapter Nineteen

A LONGING TO GO HOME

Randolph arrived early Monday morning; but unlike previous times, Rosa Lee was not ready to go. She intentionally made him wait. She was becoming irritated with his big-shot attitude and even more agitated with herself for not coming up with a plan to send him to the big house.

She watched as he exited the sky blue Caddie, took a handkerchief from his hip pocket and pretended to wipe dust from the hood. The car was already as shiny as a spanked baby's rear end, but Randolph was not about to miss a chance to impress any neighbors who might be watching.

Rosa Lee let him wait until she determined his patience were at an end before she came out of the house. "Good morning." she said. "Isn't this a beautiful day?"

"Let's go," he growled, without a good morning or even a howdy. "We're going to be late."

"I didn't know we had an appointment."

"We don't" he said, a little less arrogant; "but I have another great deal in the making. I'll, I mean the company, will make a make a good piece of change, and you'll pick up a couple of hundred too."

"Wonderful, what are we waiting for?" she replied, allowing a bit of her own attitude to show.

Randolph drove directly to the familiar parking lot where the other Cadillac was parked. "Follow me" he said and handed her the keys. "I'll not drive so fast you can't keep up."

"Drive as fast as you like, I'll be there at the same time you are. I wouldn't want you to think I don't earn my hundred dollars."

Rosa Lee unlocked the car, started the engine and waited until Patrick was a few hundred feet ahead. She pulled out of the lot, pushed hard on the accelerator and, in a moment, was right on his back bumper. That was all it took to get the feeling of revenge out of her system. She turned the radio on and tuned in a local station.

When the news' broadcaster spoke about the heirs of a local wealthy businessman, an idea hit Rosa Lee like a ton of bricks. At last, she knew exactly how she was going to arrange this hot-shot's final deal.

As she began to work out the details, the adrenalin started to flow. She moved a little closer to the rear of the blue Caddie; and at the first opportunity, she gunned the one she was driving and shot around him. When she finally pulled into the parking lot of a restaurant near the outskirts of High Point, Patrick came sliding up beside her. He jumped out of his car and his face was as red as the taillights she had shown him for the last five miles.

"What on earth were you trying to do?" he shouted.

"Find a bathroom," she replied, is a voice as calm as if she were speaking to a child.

"You could get us both locked up. Do you realize how fast you were driving?"

"They don't lock you up just for speeding, do they?"

Realizing he was about to say more than he should, Randolph begin to calm down. "No, but at that speed you could have totaled this beauty," he said while patting the hood of the automobile she was driving. "Anyway, we've almost reached our destination. We'll deliver these two babies, get back to Winston, so I can get the next deal under way."

"How are we supposed to get back to Winston?"

"There's someone waiting to take us back as we speak."

"Then we best be on our way."

"Aren't you forgetting something?"

"What?"

"The bathroom you were in such a hurry to get to."

"Oh!" She said as she rushed inside.

Just a few miles further on Randolph pulled in front of a dingy looking filling station surrounded by a thick grove of magnolia trees. A closed sign hung in a window that looked as if it hadn't been washed for at least a decade. Barely legible letters extending the entire length and just below the top edge of the building indicated the establishment had once been Miller's Garage.

Patrick parked in front of a single wide garage door that displayed a no trespassing sign. He gave three short blast on the horn. After a ten minute wait, a man whose attire perfectly matched his surroundings came from behind the building. He carried a cane which was more for show than necessity and the laces of his brogan shoes left streaks in the dust. His appearance would leave one to believe he was living in the depths of poverty, but the diamond ring on his right hand indicated otherwise. He shook hands with Patrick and was about to say something when he noticed the driver of the second Caddie was a woman.

He tapped the cane several times on the cracked pavement and turned to walk away. Patrick rushed after him. After some time, reassuring the fellow Rosa Lee could be trusted, the man opened the garage door and motioned for Patrick to pull inside. Patrick did as he was instructed just as another door opened in back of the building. Rosa Lee, not knowing what else to do followed Randolph.

When she exited the building she was completely astounded by what she saw. Four other new Cadillacs were parked side-by-side on a beautifully manicured half-acre lawn. An older automobile that Rosa Lee was certain she'd seen before was parked in front of a beautiful ranch style home. Within minutes, her suspicions were confirmed; a man whom she recognized as one of the fellows she'd seen at Randolph's place came from inside the house. He got into the familiar looking car and pulled to where Patrick and Rosa Lee were waiting. It was only after they were inside, that the stranger spoke for the first time. "Your sidekick has the necessary paperwork," and after giving Rosa Lee a suspicious stare he added, "Some day one of your old ladies is going to get us hung."

His comment made Rosa Lee so angry the hair stood up on the back of her neck. She waited for Randolph to say something in her defense, but he did not open his mouth.

"If they only knew," she thought. She sat in the back seat and stewed during the ride back to Winston and listened to Randolph and his partner in crime brag about the deal they had just made. At times, it was all she could do to refrain from lashing out; but the deal she was planning helped her remain calm.

She waited until they were almost back to Chestnut Street before setting her plan in motion. "Hey fellows, what would you say if I told you I had a friend who was in need of a couple of new automobiles?"

"Are you kidding?" Randolph asked. It was the first time he'd acknowledged she was in the car since they'd left High Point.

"Sure enough. I'm going back to the mountains for a few days but I'll let you know as soon as I have made the sale."

"You don't even know how to price one of those beauties," the driver said sarcastically.

"That's really insignificant, Sir," Rosa Lee came back. "To my friend money is no object."

"I knew I brought her on board for some reason other than just being a driver," Randolph interjected. "Here, Sweetie," he said as they came to a stop in front of Jake and Ida Mae's home. He handed her the hundred dollars she'd earned plus an extra twenty. "You stay in touch now, you hear."

"Sure enough, Randy," she said as she got out of the car and gently slammed the door.

The remainder of the evening, Rosa Lee was as excited as a teenager getting ready for her first date. She was up and down the stairs like a squirrel in a hickory tree. She kept reminding herself not to forget to pack one thing or another for her trip back to Virginia. When Ida Mae asked why she was in such a rush, she told them for the first time that she and Sidney were leaving first thing the next morning.

"Without a chaperone?" Mary Sue cried.

"Well, you can come along if you'd like."

"No, I'd probably just spoil your party."

"You're right," Rosa Lee said as she scampered back up the stairs.

The drive back to Virginia was as exciting as any either had experienced in years. It was a brisk, early October morning and evidence of the first frost still lingered on some of the darker roof tops. Halloween decorations could be seen in the windows of a few businesses near the edge of the city.

As the miles rolled away, they talked of their childhood days and the plans they'd made about spending their lives together and how one event that seemed so trivial at the time had caused their plans to be so abruptly interrupted. Rosa Lee admitted she and her mother had talked of the beautiful places they could have visited had he earned the funds needed to purchase his Model-T. She moved closer to Sidney as she told him how her mother had spoken of him right up until her passing.

With that, Sidney pulled to the side of the highway. He placed his arm around her. "There's something that has haunted me for years." he said. "If I had not run away, I'm sure I would have spent time in jail. Would you have waited?"

She laid her head on his shoulder. "Let's pretend I'm still waiting," she whispered. Sidney held her close and kissed her for the first time in more than forty years. A young lady in a passing car gave a friendly wave and the driver gave a short blast on the horn.

"What are you doing," Rosa Lee teased, "giving me such a passionate kiss in the middle of the day and parked on the side of a busy highway?"

"Oh, I guess I got carried away; please say you will forgive me."

"Only if you'll get carried away one more time," she coaxed.

Sidney accepted the challenge before pulling back onto the pavement.

Soon they were north of Mt. Airy and crossing into Virginia. As they began the climb up the mountain, signs of fall became more evident. Hand-painted posters advertising merchandise available at roadside markets just ahead lined the highway. Baskets of freshly picked apples of all species, sizes, and colors stacked along side huge piles of pumpkins were everywhere.

"Wouldn't it be great if we could live as these folks do?" Sidney asked.

"Selling pumpkins?"

"Not just pumpkins, Honey, all sorts of produce: corn, string beans, carrots, radishes, beets, and anything else the rich soil on a mountain farm would produce."

"You, a judge, wanting to be a farmer?"

"Why not, I became a lawyer because of the need to earn a living, a judgeship just seemed to follow. What I would really like is farming with cattle, pigs, chickens, and one billy goat."

"You're serious, aren't you?"

"Sure I am."

"Then what on earth would you want with one billy goat?"

"To remind me of how hardheaded I was for allowing you to get away from me."

Rosa Lee gave him a big smile before commenting, "You purchase a farm, and I'll buy the goat."

It was nearing suppertime by the time they reached the top of a high ridge that separated the counties where their families lived. Sidney parked beside the county line marker and invited Rosa Lee to go for a walk. They strolled hand-in-hand for several hundred feet along a well traveled path until they reached a clearing. A large circle of stones lay on one side of the trail and a much smaller circle on the other. Each circle encompassed the remnants of a bonfire. Rosa Lee hesitated, wanting to inquire as to the meaning of the stones but Sidney nudged her ahead toward a well constructed wooden platform. When they were a distance away from the structure he ask her to close her eyes. She did as she was told and allowed him to lead her onto the platform. When she opened her eyes the view was absolutely breathtaking. The platform was built on the edge of a cliff and positioned in such a manner that allowed one to see for miles.

She stood for a moment grasping Sidney's hand for fear she might be in danger of falling onto the treetops below. When she realized she was in no danger she released her companion's hand and ventured to the handrail at the edge of the construction.

"Do you see anything you recognize," he asked.

"No, should I?"

"Keep looking."

"Oh no! that's our house, and over there is the Baxter farm," she screamed, pointing to all the places she was able to identify. "How long have you known about this place?"

"Only about fifty years, I'd say."

"Why have I never heard of it?"

"Well, to tell the truth few ladies do. It's supposed to be sort of a getaway for the fellows in this area. This is where they come to when they go coon hunting. Some do a good bit of hunting and a little drinking, occasionally, some of the fellows forget which comes first. For years this place was known only to us men folks. Then one day it happened, old man Johnson stayed out two days longer than his coon dog then went home smelling of whiskey. He had no idea Mrs. Johnson would follow him the very next time she allowed him to go hunting. He begged her not to tell about their hunting camp but as you can guess the word got out."

"What do the two circles of stones signify?"

"Oh, that. The large circle is where the old timers sit and brag about how many coons they've caught while the younger fellows do the actual hunting. When a young fellow is old enough to begin hunting he is required to sit by himself until he can buy or trade for a dog good enough to tree a coon before any of the other hounds."

"You never told me you like to coon hunt."

"I didn't, but I sure liked to come up here, look down on the farm where you lived and dream."

"You're awesome."

"I know," he smiled. "Could we discuss that further tomorrow? Right now I need to get you home. I have reservations at Fuller's Hotel, and I wouldn't want them to think I'm not going to make it."

Sidney drove the short distance to Ira's place where they found Mary Ellen and the twins waiting.

Rosa Lee could hardly wait for Sidney to get out of the car so she could introduce him to the family. "Sidney," she said, as soon as they were close enough to be heard, "this wonderful lady is my daughter-in-law Mary Ellen."

"I'm so pleased to finally meet you," Mary Ellen told him, "and I am so grateful to you for being lenient when passing sentence on Mary Sue and J.D. I'm sure they've both learned their lesson."

Before either of them could say more, Rosa Lee introduced Sidney to the twins, Kervin and Kevin. "These bright young fellows will be graduating in the spring and they would both like to be farmers."

"Boy, do we have a lot to talk about," Sidney told them as he seated himself in front of them on the edge of the porch.

"Well," Mary Ellen said jokingly, "I guess he told us. Let's go fix something to eat."

The judge and the twins plunged into a conversation about farming that lasted for the next two hours. In fact, when Rosa Lee brought a tray with three large glasses of tea, they barely shut up long enough to say thanks. The judge did take just long enough to ask her to call the hotel and tell them he'd be late but to please hold his room.

"Yes, Sir, Your Honor," she said, but he was already so engrossed in listening to the twins he hadn't even heard.

A half-hour later a "supper time" call came just as Ira's cruiser pulled to a stop in front of the yard gate. It didn't take long to get all the men folk seated around the table; and, to no surprise to anyone, the ladies had proved once again how well they could cook.

When they finished eating, Sidney said good night. He and Rosa Lee agreed to wait a couple days before getting back together. She felt she needed to catch up on all the happenings since she'd been away, and the ladies club meeting the following day was just the place to do it. Sidney also needed some time. He wanted to go back to his home place and try to locate some of his old acquaintances.

Chapter Twenty

PLANNING PATRICK'S DOWNFALL

Rosa Lee was amazed to learn all that had happened while she was away. The day after Baxter's arrest he began making plans to clear himself. He intended to place all the blame on the Sutters but he soon learned that was not to be. He ordered the Sutters to vacate immediately; hoping they would go back to the hills of West Virginia and be lost forever. Ira, however, was a step ahead of him once more. Every member of the Sutter family had already been issued summons and ordered not to leave the state.

It took all his ready cash to make bail; and he knew, if he were to have any chance of staying out of prison, he was going to have to hire the best lawyers in the state. To do so, he would have to raise as much cash as possible; and he needed to do it at once. His only hope was to put his farm up for sale. Within forty-eight hours of making bail, he had his property in the hands of a realtor.

While Sidney busied himself trying to find some of the old boys he had grown up with, Rosa Lee set out on a mission of her own. She had Ira take her to Cleveland so she could visit her old friend down on the Clinch. In spite of the sheriff's insistence that he drive all the way to Gertie's home, she chose to walk along the tracks. It was exciting for her to watch the bass, redeye and blue-

Granny's Justice

gill rise to the water's surface to gulp the insects that fell among the leaves.

A hundred yards from Gertie's home Rosa Lee could smell burning wood. Since it was an unusually warm morning there was no need to heat her home, so Rosa Lee was sure Gertie was preserving food for the winter. Moments later her suspicions were confirmed. Gertie was sitting in a ladder-back chair stirring in a large black kettle almost filled with apple butter. A container of McCormick cinnamon lay on her lap. A pile of short hickory limbs to fuel the fire beneath the kettle lay within her reach. Her head was slightly bowed, and the stirring motion was in perfect rhythm with the barely audible singing of her favorite hymn. Bingo lay beside her chair completely unaware of Rosa Lee's presence.

Rosa Lee moved within feet of her without being detected. She hesitated for a moment, overcome by a feeling of sympathy. She waited for the beginning of the next chorus then joined in. Immediately the singing turned into a hardy hello.

"What brings you to this neck of the woods?" Gertie asked.

"I brought you a good looking feller to help you with all the chores around here. I got him hidden down by the river."

"Then, hurry down there and push him in. I can take care of these little chores without having to take care of some know-it-all old man trying to tell me how to do things his way." Rosa Lee quickly remembered she need not harbor any sympathy for this spunky old lady.

"How have you been?" Rosa Lee asked, giving Gertie a gentle embrace.

"If I was any better, I couldn't stand it."

"I'm sorry to hear that, honey; I need for you to be seriously ill."

"Say what?"

"In fact, I need for you to be so bad off you're getting your departing papers in order."

"Rosa Lee Duncan, have you taken leave of your senses, or has somebody been beating on you with a silly stick? Anyhow, all

I own is this old riverside farm; and a little sum of cash I keep in an old butter churn."

"Are you going to leave all you own to your two young'ns?"

"Honey, we got to get you to a doctor. You know I ain't got no young'ns."

Rosa Lee selected another chair from off the back porch, took the stirring ladle from Gertie. "Let me give you a break and explain what I'm talking about before you really think I'm crazy," Rosa Lee laughed.

"I believe it's too late, dear; but why don't you give it a try?"

"Remember the guy I was telling you about, the car salesman down in North Carolina?"

"Oh yes, Honey, I remember, your knight in shining armor."

"Well, he's not the fellow I thought he was. The truth is, he's a crook. He steals cars, usually Cadillacs, from dealers all over the state and sells them to other crooks who don't mind them having a fake title. Some of them, he tears apart and sells parts on the black market."

"You're not going to tell me he's gotten you involved?"

"Well, sorta. You might say."

"Why don't you tell the authorities?"

"The authorities are watching him, but I want to be the one to send him up the river. The next time he sets out to use some unsuspecting female to assist him in his illegal ventures, I want the name Rosa Lee Duncan to bounce around in his head like a pea in a whistle."

"How do you figure on doing that?"

"I want you to buy a couple of his Cadillacs."

"You what? I really like you a lot, dear; but if you don't mind I'd just as soon not spend my final days working on a chain gang."

"Let me tell what I have in mind. I'm going to tell this hoodlum you're a friend who is at death's door and you want to do something really special for your two sons. They both like to impress the young girls, kinda act big shot, you know what I mean, just a little above their rais'un."

"Not my boys; I taught them better than to do a thing like that," Gertie interrupted, giggling.

"Will you be quiet, Gertie, and let me finish my story?"

"Well if you're going to spin that big a yarn, I should at least be allowed to add a little fib or two."

"To continue with my story, you figure if you left each of them a new Cadillac, they would be a step or two above other guys that might be some competition."

"Now ain't that nice of me to treat my boys so good?" Gertie went on. "When am I supposed to purchase these new automobiles?"

"Next week, if I can arrange it."

"Gracious, I must be worse off than the doctor told me. If I'm that bad off you better rush this deal along, I might not last two weeks."

Rosa Lee was beginning to get a might baffled, but she allowed Gertie to have her fun. "In fact, you are too weak to travel, so he will have to deliver the Caddies right here to your door."

"Then what?"

"Since you're my closest friend, I'll be driving one of the cars myself. Your boys are really going to be surprised."

"Me too." Gertie could not contain her laughter any longer.

"Why will you be surprised?" Rosa Lee asked.

"What?? You'll be doing what? You can't even drive a horse to water and you're telling me you can drive a Cadillac."

"Gertie, if you don't quit interrupting, I'll have to get another one of my friends to help me pull this off."

"Wow, are you telling me all your friends are getting ready to kick the bucket? I believe if I were you, I'd start hanging out with some younger folks. By the way, when am I going to meet these two boys of mine, and can you believe I can't even remember their names?" Then, getting serious, she allowed Rosa Lee to continue.

Although a sense of anger was about to flare up, Rosa Lee thought of how crazy all this must sound to her old friend and managed a big smile.

"Those two good looking sons of yours will here be the day the Caddies are delivered, and their names are Ira and Howard."

Suddenly Gertie realized this lady really had plans. She remembered how their tape recording had been the instrument that brought about Baxter's downfall; now, she felt honored that her friend had chosen her to aid in bringing another criminal to justice. "Do the fellows know about this?"

"No, but they will if you agree to help me"

"Count me in, just tell what I need to do," Gertie offered.

"Just continue to be your onery self' I'll let you know what day this will take place. I'll have Ira get you the money to pay for the automobiles."

"That won't be necessary; it can't be more than a few thousand. I'll just take it out of the churn."

"Son of a gun, Gertie, when this is over will you call me the next time you get ready to make butter?"

Gertie just grinned, "If you'll help me get this apple butter in those jars over there, we'll go inside and have a bowl of my homemade stew."

"That's what smelled so good as I came up to your house. How could anyone resist a deal like that? I'll fill the jars, and you can tighten the lids."

Rosa Lee watched as Gertie made the third attempt to get out of her chair before she was able to stand. She could not help noticing how frail her friend appeared as she moved to the table that held the canning jars.

"Gertie, are you okay?"

"You bet. Why do you ask?"

"Gertie, I'm not blind; you are so weak you can hardly walk. Have you seen a doctor?"

"Oh yeah, he said I was getting old, gave me a huge bottle of vitamins, said I should feel much better in a few days."

* * * * * *

It took a little doing but Rosa Lee convinced Ira she would be in no danger before he would agree to help her set the trap. Once she had everything in place, she could hardly wait to get back to Winston. She was going to let this hot-shot know he was not the only one who could sell cars. It fact, she decided she was going to ask for an additional fifty dollars for making the transaction. She smiled thinking where he was going, he wouldn't need much cash anyway.

Rosa Lee asked if Sidney had called or been by while she was at Gertie's. Ira told her no, but he had seen him in town every day.

"If you see him again, please tell him to come get me."

"Getting a little anxious, Mom?"

"Yeahhhhhhh, Buddy!"

Ira got word to Sidney, who called Rosa Lee the next morning. She was surprised he was not ready to get back to North Carolina. Instead, he wanted her to meet some of his childhood friends who were still living on the farms where they had lived when they were children. It was a joyous day for Sidney, and she too would have enjoyed it more had it not been overshadowed by her anxiety to get her plan under way. Sidney knew nothing of her plans, and she was careful to make sure he had no part in it. If anything went wrong the blame must fall solely on her.

The next morning, Sidney came by for breakfast, and Rosa Lee hardly recognized him. He was dressed in a pair of blue jeans, a checkered flannel shirt and wore a felt hat that he deposited on the porch swing on his way inside. He, Ira, and the twins, talked of nothing but farming as they put away at least a dozen of Mary Ellen's homemade biscuits covered with redeye gravy. Several slices of sugar-cured ham, a platter of eggs, and a large pot of coffee also disappeared.

When they'd finished eating the judge pushed back from the table and loosened his belt a couple notches. "Mary Ellen," he said, "I had almost forgotten how good country cooking tasted. If you'd promise to invite me to breakfast at least once a month, I'd move back to the mountains."

Rosa Lee, who had rushed through her meal, was so anxious to get started back to Winston she could hardly sit still. She asked Sidney at least three times if he was ready to leave as he was finishing his last cup of coffee. The family could not believe she was in such a hurry to leave the mountain. In fact, they could not remember ever seeing her so excited to do anything.

Ira escorted his mother to the car while the judge was bidding farewell to Mary Ellen and the twins. "Be careful Mom," he warned. "I have no jurisdiction anywhere but here in the county; but if anything should go wrong . . ."

"Nothing is going to go wrong. You just make sure you and Howard are down on the river when we deliver those two Cadillacs."

"We'll be there; and if you pull this off, I think I'll put you on as my chief investigator."

"No, thanks! When I get out of the automobile business I think I'll retire and settle down with Jake and Ida Mae down in the Carolinas."

"But, Mom, you can't do that. You could never be happy living in the city. You belong with us here in the mountains. I know we're a little crowded; but if we can make it through the winter, I'll add a couple more rooms come spring. The twins are getting to be quite a muscular pair of young men. With their help, I'll have it done in no time."

"Nonsense, I enjoy living with Jake and the girls, but I admit I miss the wide open spaces we had on Baxter's place. What's happening with him anyway?"

"Oh, he's out on bond, bragging about how he was framed. I heard someone bought his farm, so I suppose he's got enough money to pay his high-priced lawyers. I'm sure he thinks he's smart enough to get off. I'm betting he'll be a long time gone."

Ira wanted to ask her if she knew how long it would be before she would be delivering the automobiles Gertie had purchased; but Sidney, Mary Ellen, and the boys were too near to continue the conversation.

"You'll be back right away, won't you, Granny?" Mary Ellen asked. "The Harvest Festival is the first weekend in November. I'm sure you wouldn't want to miss it, and we need to make plans for our family reunion, too. Maybe you could talk Sidney into joining us if he has no other plans."

"Yeah! That sounds like a super idea. What do you say, Your Honor?" Kervin added. "We still have a lot more farming ideas to discuss, and every farm machinery dealer for miles around will be displaying their newest equipment at the festival."

"I was speaking about our reunion," his mother reminded him.

"Yeah, you could come to that, too, if want to."

"Could be. I'll take it under advisement."

"He'll be there," Rosa Lee said without hesitation.

The judge smiled as he shifted the car into gear and moved onto the highway.

Chapter Twenty-One

THE DOUBLE-CROSS

Upon arriving in Winston, Rosa Lee wasted no time putting her plan into action. She called Randolph, totally excited about having an order for two brand new Cadillacs. She was very specific about the details. They were to be dark blue, with chrome wheels and fender skirts; and they needed to be delivered to the buyer in exactly two weeks. She was adamant about the delivery date, stating that her friend was on her way out, and the automobiles were to be her last gifts to her two sons.

Randolph was overwhelmed by the interest Rosa Lee was taking in the business. He felt he had her exactly where he wanted her. She was becoming so deeply involved with his transactions she would be afraid not to do whatever he asked of her. He assured her he would have the Caddies she described and the delivery date would not be a problem.

Now that she had set the trap, all she had to do was wait for the prey to take the bait. In the meantime, she busied herself spending time with Sidney. After their trip back to Virginia, the judge talked of little else but his desire to spend his sunset years back in the mountains. Rosa Lee had to admit she was growing tired of city life. "I feel as if I'm living on 'God's Little Acre'," she told Sidney one afternoon while they were parked at an overlook above the city of Mt. Airy.

"You really miss living on a farm, don't you?" he asked.

Rosa Lee snuggled close to Sidney, lay her head on his shoulder and poured out her heart. She told of how she and Ira's father had dreams of owning a farm but the nearest they had ever come was living as sharecroppers. They had moved from farm to farm until at last their dream had became a nightmare. When he had passed on and she had moved in with Ira, she once again cherished the wide open spaces a big farm offered. That, too, came to an abrupt end, and she had given up on the idea of ever having freshly tilled soil squish between her toes as she gently placed vegetable seed into the ground.

"Do you really believe the twins would be happy farming for a living?"

"They wouldn't be happy doing anything else. Many days they sit on the porch and stare at the Baxter farm where they grew up. I think, like me, they are suffering from claustrophobia. It has even grown worse since the 'For Sale' signs have been removed. No one in the community seems to know who bought the place, but I'll bet they got a real bargain because he needed to raise money in a hurry. You really like the twins, don't you, Sidney?"

"I sure do. I don't believe I've ever met young men of their age who knew exactly what they wanted to do. They love farming and the idea of being their own boss. I do believe they'll be successful one day."

"Do you think we can come back for the festival?" Rosa Lee asked.

"We have to; you promised, you know, Ms. Boss."

"It sure is a good feeling," Rosa Lee added.

"What?"

"Being able to tell a judge what to do."

Sidney smiled, "You like that, do you?"

For the next two weeks, the two were almost inseparable. Sidney was there by midmorning every day to take Rosa Lee shopping, to see some new sight or some new place to eat. Each day as he stopped in front of her house, Rosa Lee was like a young teenager going on her first date. Each evening when she came home, she told how they both talked of moving back to the mountains.

"Together, Granny?" Mary Sue asked one evening.

"That would be nice," Rosa Lee admitted, but added the judge had never mentioned the idea.

"Then what does he talk about every day?"

"Farming."

"If he talks of nothing but farming, be thankful he doesn't mention moving back together," Mary Sue joked as she bounded up the stairs to bed.

It was true that Sidney and Granny talked about farming, the twins, and moving back to Virginia. The only topic she did not discuss was the deal with Gertie. She was afraid he would not approve. If all went well, it wouldn't matter anyway.

It was only two days until the delivery date, and she was getting a little uneasy. She was more than a little uneasy; she was almost paranoid. Could Randy have somehow become aware of her relationship with Sidney or simply become suspicious? Anyway, time was running out; and she was really nervous . During dinner two days before the date of the sale, she got the call that set her mind at ease.

"How's my number one sales' lady?" It was Randolph all right, using his over complimentary hypocritical voice. "Got the two chariots you requested, in the color you wanted, ready for delivery tomorrow. You did tell the old nag it would be cash, of course."

Rosa Lee's anger rose so quickly, she could almost feel fire shoot from the top of her head like from a smoke stack on top of a brick oven. Her first thought was to tell him where to go and that he could use one of those stolen cars as a means of transportation; but she regained her composure.

"Out of the question! She gave me explicit instruction about the day to deliver and that's day after tomorrow. That's the day she'll have the cash, and the day she's told her sons to be at her home. If I try to tell her otherwise, she'll cancel the order and go elsewhere."

"Whatever you say; but it means I'll have to postpone an important engagement."

"I'll see you the day after tomorrow morning. Pick me up early. She's expecting us at noon, and I've told her we will be there."

"If that's the way the old biddy wants it" he said and hung up.

She could hardly wait until the line was clear so she could call Ira.

"Hi, Son, can you and Howard be at Gertie's house at noon day after tomorrow? Wonderful, I'll see you then."

The next day she gave Sidney some excuse as to why she would be unable to see him for a couple of days. Now, all she had to do was wait.

Patrick arrived early as was customary on days he was going to make an illegal dollar. He was driving one of the Cadillacs which matched the description she had given him to a tee. Within minutes, they were at the parking lot behind the vacant warehouse where the stolen cars were kept. "I assume you've made arrangements for us to get back to Winston."

"Sure have, my boy will give us a ride."

"Marvelous, now where are we taking these beauties?"

"I'll follow you until we reach the state line and then I'll go in front." In order to make the deal sound legit she added. "You do remember I get an extra hundred dollars for this sale."

"I remember, dear. Let's not keep the old crab waiting."

Rosa Lee was so mad as she followed him out of the parking lot she wanted to drive her automobile right up his exhaust pipe, but she decided she could hold her temper for at least another few hours. She was not prone to cursing, but the few words she mumbled to herself could not have been uttered in the presence of her pastor.

She followed Patrick out of Winston as they headed north. She would normally have been right on his bumper, but today she chose to lag behind, barely keeping him in sight. She did so for no other reason than to annoy him. He'd slow down long enough for her to catch up then set down hard on the gas; and in a little while, he'd lose her again. She continued driving like that until they crossed into Virginia. They were no more than a hundred yards past the state line when Randolph pulled to the side of the road. By the time Rosa Lee caught up he was already out of his car waiting for her.

"What's holding you up?" he snapped.

"Oh, I'm sorry, I guess I was just enjoying the scenery."

"I thought you said the old lady wanted these cars at exactly noon today."

Rosa Lee could tell that inside Patrick was so angry he could bite the heads of nails off, but she pretended not to notice.

"If we are a little late, I'm sure she won't mind. Our favorite restaurant is just up ahead let's stop for breakfast."

"You are joking, aren't you?"

"Of course not, I'm hungry."

"All right, but if this deal falls through, I'm going to be one hot Jose!"

"Trust me dear, I assure you everything will go as planned,. We'll grab a quick bite and be on our way."

Rosa Lee followed Randolph the remaining few miles to Mama's Home Cooking restaurant. Once inside she headed straight to the table where she had sat the day he introduced himself. The place had very few customers, so Irene was there to take their order almost immediately.

"I'll have the special," Rosa Lee told her.

"Just coffee," Randolph said. " We're sort of in a hurry," he added.

"Better have something; we still have a three hour drive you know."

"I can see the automobile business must be good these days," Irene commented as she placed their order on the table.

"Couldn't be better," Rosa Lee was quick to answer. She gave Irene a quick wink while her companion was reaching for the sugar bowl.

When she determined she had agitated Randolph enough, she rushed through her breakfast and asked for the check.

"Oh, no, it's on the house," Irene insisted.

"I told you that you should have something," Rosa Lee joked.

Moments later, they were on their way.

Rosa Lee drove as fast as the law would allow until she reached the outskirts of Cleveland. She was sure not to drive over the twenty-five miles per hour speed limit through town, just in case there might be someone who would recognize her and want to wave hello. No such luck however, the streets were almost deserted as was the case in most small towns on a weekday.

Rosa Lee stopped on the bank of the river near the railroad crossing. She got out of her car and walked to the side of the one Randolph was driving. "Here we are," she said.

"What do you mean 'Here we are'? the only living creatures I've seen in this town are one old man and two pigeons. I'm pretty certain all three of them are asleep. I'll wager there isn't enough money in this whole town to buy two fine automobiles like these."

Rosa Lee looked across the street at the railroad depot. Sure enough, there on one of the park benches was the local hobo, Wally "No Toes' Hackney. He had been a hobo for as long as anyone could remember. He'd come into town on one of the freight cars, hang around for a week or so, then one day he'd be gone. No one ever knew where he went or if he'd ever be back; but most folks knew how he got his nickname. It happened near the depot one Saturday afternoon when the streets were crowded. Wally was leaving town; and as he ran along side one of the box cars and was ready to jump on board his foot slipped. It went right under one of those big iron wheels. Some folks say you could hear his scream above the roar of the locomotive. The accident had him laid up for a few weeks, but it did not change his mode of travel.

Rosa Lee turned her Caddie onto the narrow graveled area that lay parallel to the tracks. "Follow me," she called back to Randolph.

"Are you crazy?" he yelled.

"That's beside the point. If you want to turn these Caddies into cash, you better follow me."

"This old bat must live in a cave." he mumbled. "Let's go."

As Rosa Lee drove the remaining half-mile, she got so excited she was loosing her grip on the steering wheel. She drove right over the ends of the crossties allowing a cloud of black coal dust to all but cover the windshield of the car behind her. When she stopped in front of Gertie's house, Randolph bailed out of his car and hurried up to where Rosa Lee was waiting for him.

"I believe you should have sold your friend a couple of horses and buggies instead of these babies." He hadn't even noticed Gertie who was sitting in her rocking chair at the far end of her porch. "Is that her?" he whispered.

"Yep"

"Wonderful. Let's get this deal closed so we can get out of here."

Rosa Lee led Patrick onto the porch and made the necessary introductions. "Pleased to meet you Ma'am. Sorry to hear about your illness, and I must say this is one of the most gracious acts of kindness I've seen in some time. My assistant did inform you that at these prices most of my company's transaction are cash only."

"Of course, I understand completely. Is the paper work in order?"

"Right here, Ma'am, just insert the names of your two well-deserving sons; and your local titling office will take care of any final paper work."

Gertie slipped a large envelope from her apron pocket and handed it to Patrick.

He placed the envelope in his hip pocket without taking time to look inside. "I was looking forward to meeting the lucky young men. I'm really sorry they are not here."

"I wouldn't think of disappointing you, sir. Boys! Hey, Boys!"

Granny's Justice

"I'm right here," Ira said as he stepped onto the porch.

"I'm here too, " Howard echoed as he stepped out directly behind the sheriff. Both officers were in full uniform.

"Randy, dear, I'd like you to meet my son, Sheriff Ira Duncan and his Chief Deputy Howard Barton."

Patrick's face turned the color of chalk, as he began to stutter. "You've set me up, woman.! You didn't tell me your son was a cop."

"You didn't bother to tell me you were one of the biggest car thieves in the country either. I also didn't tell me he was a jeweler, but I'm guessing he has a set of bracelets that's just your size, right, Sheriff?"

"Right. Would you like to do the honors, Deputy?"

"Turn around and place your hands behind your back sir. You are under arrest."

Howard escorted Patrick to the back of the house where two squad cars were carefully hidden. "Great work ladies; and just for the record, Baxter has chosen to take the advice of his high-priced attorney and accept a plea bargain. I suppose he'll be back on the streets in a few years, but he'll be well supervised for a long time to come."

"Ever hear who bought the farm, son?"

"Sorry, Mother, I haven't heard a word. Are you ready to go now that you ladies have wrapped up your most high priority case?"

"Would you stay with me tonight please, Rosie? You wouldn't mind having someone come pick her up tomorrow, would you, Sheriff?"

"How could I say no to two of the finest detectives in the entire county? I'll have someone come get these automobiles tomorrow; and I'll have your cash back to you within the week."

Chapter Twenty-Two

AN ACT OF KINDNESS

Rosa Lee sat on the porch with Gertie until far past sundown. They talked of how dangerous it could have been helping put two crooks behind bars. They talked of how life was becoming more difficult as the years flew by; then as the reflection of a full moon began showing it face in the still waters below, Gertie began reminiscing about her life on the Clinch. It was as if she were looking into her past as she stared at the river. In a soft, gentle voice, she seemed to be penning the pages of a book that would be shared by the handful of people whose lives she had touched.

Rosa Lee silently listened to her friend tell how she and her husband Herman came to settle on the banks of the river. Her story began when she was a young girl growing up in a small town in the state of West Virginia. It, too, was located near one of the best fishing streams in the entire state. The Tug was known far and wide for producing more trophy catches than any stream its size in the whole south.

Gertrude, Gertie to her friends, was a miracle child of parents who were married late in life. Her mother was a devout Christian and spent most of her time doing charity work with other ladies in the congregation. Her father was a coal miner and devoted almost as much time to fishing the Tug as her mother did with her charity work. He was known for being able to catch more and bigger large mouth bass than any man in the county.

Gertie, more or less a tomboy, chose to spend all of her free time with her father. Many days during her childhood, she spent hours digging earthworms or catching grasshoppers which she and her daddy used as bait when he got home from work. He always came home covered with black coal dust, but as quickly as he took his bath, he and Gertie would head for the river. If the signs were right for catching the big ones, he would sometimes skip his bath to have more time fishing. If it were during the summer, he would send Gertie on home; and he would bathe in the river. This practice was never mentioned anywhere, but in the privacy of their own home and then only because her mother gave him a good dressing down each time it happened.

"Aren't you afraid the neighbors will see you?"

"Not unless they can see in the dark," was always her daddy's answer.

It was during one of those days while fishing on the Tug that she met Herman. She was in her late teens, and many summer days while her mother was busying herself doing good deeds, Gertie would be on the banks of the river. One early afternoon in September, the bass were grabbing almost everything she threw into the water, and Gertie was having the time of her life. All at once she saw a large fish come out of the water about a hundred yards upstream. At the same time she heard someone yell, "You won't get away this time, baby!"

She slowly made her way to where the voice came from but still could not see to whom the voice belonged. Suddenly, the tall weeds parted and a good looking young man stepped out right in front of her. He was holding the biggest small mouth bass she had ever seen.

"He sure is a whopper," Gertie told him. "What did you catch him on?"

"Macaroni."

"Macaroni? I've never heard of anyone using macaroni for fish bait. Why were you hiding in those weeds?"

"Where I came from I would have been punished had I been caught digging worms. We had macaroni at least four times a week, so it was easy for me to share some of my dinner with the fish."

As Herman told the story of his young life, a lasting relationship began to develop. He said he was an orphan, living in a home for children like himself. The orphanage was way down south on a Louisiana bayou. The population of the home was over a hundred and was well supervised. It was surrounded by a tall wire fence, and no one was allowed to leave without an adult chaperone. The number of instructors and adult supervisors was very limited, so permission to leave was seldom granted. The fence served two purposes: the first, was to keep residents inside; the second was to keep them safe from alligators and other wild animals.

One day Herman was watching an old man who was fishing a short distance from the orphanage. He was catching a fish with almost every cast. What he was doing seemed like so much fun Herman decided to go talk with him. He managed to unravel enough wire at the bottom of the fence to slide underneath. He told the old gentleman the truth about being one of the orphans and that he would never be allowed to go fishing. From that day forward the two formed a lasting friendship. At least three days every week, Herman would slide under the fence; and he and the old man would go fishing. He was always afraid of being caught, so he was careful to hide among the weeds and brush that grew along the river. That's why he was so well hidden when Gertie first heard him call out.

A few weeks later, the old man didn't show up nor ever again. Herman learned he had died from a massive heart attack. Their days of fishing together had come to an end. A short time later, he went under the fence for the last time. He headed north, sleeping in barns, eating handouts, and catching rides with whoever would allow him to do so. One day he ended up living with a family on the banks of the Tug. Two years later we were married; and a short time later we headed out to find some where we could buy a small place of our own and be able to go fishing any time we had a mind to. That's how we found our way here to the Clinch.

It was at the end of her story that Gertie took her eyes from the river and began talking directly to Rosa Lee. "There's one more thing I want to tell you, dear. As I have told you, Herman was an orphan; and we had no children of our own. It's so ironic you told me a few days ago that I was at death's door, because you were more correct than you knew. I have seen a doctor as I told you, but it was not vitamins he prescribed, it was a warning that I needed to get ready to leave the river. My heart is growing weaker, and I might leave any day now."

Tears began to well up in Rosa Lee's eyes. She opened her mouth to speak, but Gertie raised her hand to silence her. "Everything here on the river and what savings I have will be given to the Salvation Army. All my funeral arrangements have been made and this, my dear, is yours." She reached into her apron pocket and removed folded legal document. As Rosa Lee read tears began to fall from her face onto the paper. It was the deed to the Baxter farm giving ownership to one Lee Wilcox. Rosa Lee fell to her knees, lay her head on Gertie's lap and sobbed as she had never done before.

"Why me?" she asked.

"Because you are so deserving. I had Howard help me find out your maiden name so Baxter nor the real-estate agent would know who was buying his property. I must say the transaction went off without a hitch. The deed has not yet been recorded so no one can find out who the new owner might be. Now if you will help me out of this rocking chair, we'll go to bed."

Rosa Lee helped Gertie into bed, then went to the guest room across the hall. She tossed and turned until way past midnight, listening to the gentle snoring from across the way. She lay for hours debating who should be the first to know about her good fortune.

She'd never owned more than enough soil to fill a flower pot; now she was the proprietor of one of the largest farms in the county.

The moonlight shown brightly upon the waters of the Clinch and crept silently into her bedroom. An hour short of daybreak, the gentle roar of an approaching freight train drowned the sound of Gertie's snoring. Soon the rattle of couplings and the movement of well-greased wheels grinding on the rails vibrated through the dwelling. When the last car screeched past and the hum of the locomotive faded, an almost ghostly feeling filled Rosa Lee's bedroom. A voice, so gentle, barely above a whisper, yet so audible, pierced the silence.

"Are you awake, Rosie?"

"Yes, Ma'am."

"Do you think there'll be some place to fish when we get to Heaven?"

"You bet."

At the first crack of dawn, Rosa Lee was awakened by the sound of Gertie's rooster. The chill of an early fall morning filled the air. She slipped out of bed and tiptoed into the kitchen. She chose a few sticks of kindling from the wood box and placed them on the smoldering embers in the cook stove. She dipped two scoops of coffee from the grinder, took stock of the quantity then dashed in another half scoop; a little extra chicory would get the blood circulating.

There had not been a sound from Gertie's room, but Rosa Lee knew the smell of fresh morning brew would bring her from under the covers. When she determined the coffee was at it peak, she took two cups from the warming closet, poured a cup for each of them and waited to hear footsteps. Still there was not a sound. She stepped to the door of Gertie's room and called, "One or two, fried or scrambled?"

When there was no answer, Rosa Lee rushed to her friend's bedside and laid a hand on her shoulder. The cold rigid form beneath her touch caused her to tremble. Gertie couldn't be gone, not like this. Rosa Lee was no stranger to death, but she had never felt so alone. She sat for a while, stroking the hand of her departed friend, bewildered by the mixed emotions churning inside her. On the one hand, she felt eternally grateful that Gertie's last earthly deed was to fulfill Rosa Lee's dream of owning a place of her own. On the other, she was almost angry at her for leaving so abruptly, giving her no opportunity to show her appreciation.

Sometime near mid-morning, she walked the railroad into Cleveland and asked the store proprietor to call the sheriff's office. She told Ira what had happened and asked him to have the funeral home come for Gertie's body and to have Howard come take her home.

"I'll come for you, Mom," Ira insisted.

"No, have Howard do it, please; and tell him to say nothing about Gertie's affairs. You might also tell him Bingo will be riding in the back seat."

Chapter Twenty-Three

THE EVENT OF THE YEAR

The three-day Fall Harvest Festival drew crowds second only to the county fair. Vendors from all over the county gathered to display their wares. Large banners were used to draw attention to the merchandise being displayed. Crafters demonstrating their goods lined the perimeter of the festival area. The smell of popcorn, pork barbecue, pans of boiling molasses, and bubbling apple butter filled the air.

The sound of the muskets being fired by Civil War reenactors echoed through the adjacent woods. The clang of horseshoes being tossed around steel pegs indicated the most talked about tournament in the county was under way. The two dollar entry fee required from each of the many contestants insured the winning couple a sizeable purse.

Almost everyone in the county attended the festival, and the Duncan family was no exception. Ida Mae and Mary Sue came up from Winston; and John Robert, from Norfolk. Mary Ellen took pride in being escorted by her husband, the sheriff.

The female members of the Duncan family spent time admiring art work, watching crafters such as jewelry makers, broom makers, and basket weavers at work. They ate kettle corn, sampled the many offerings of cakes, candies, and other assorted goodies.

John Robert and the twins' interest was taking place on the east end of the festival grounds. They enjoyed the performance of the Civil War reenactors and took their turns at being eliminated in the horseshoe tournament. However, their main interest was the turkey shoot. The rules were quite simple. A large wooden crate containing a turkey was placed fifty yards from a white line. The crate had a hole in the top, and the turkey was constantly pushing his head through the hole. For the small sum of one half-dollar a contestant was permitted to take one shot with a musket rifle. If the musket ball brought blood from the rapidly moving head of the turkey, the bird belonged to him. The fellows watched as one contestant after the other loaded the rifle but failed to claim the turkey. When the last man took his turn and missed, Kervin asked if he could be allowed to have a turn.

"Certainly," the man in charge agreed.

Kervin stepped to the line and asked for a musket ball. He was given the ball, but he didn't pick up the rifle. Instead he removed his slingshot from his hip pocket and placed the musket ball in the leather pouch. After waiting for the snickers to subside, he took careful aim. When he released the ball, the turkey's head disappeared. The fellow in charge approached the crate and peeped through the hole.

"It appears the young man is going to have turkey for Thanksgiving dinner."

All of a sudden the snickers became cheers.

Rosa Lee tried as best she could to enjoy the festivities but her heart was not really in it. It had been barely two weeks since Gertie had been laid to rest beside her beloved Herman on a knoll near the banks of the river she loved so well. Only she and Howard knew about Gertie's good deed and she knew Howard was going to explode if she postponed telling her family for much longer. She, too, was anxious to share the news, but she wanted it to be at exactly the right moment.

Early on Saturday morning, the second day of the festival, three of the ladies got an unexpected surprise. When they arrived at the main gate Jake, J.D. and Sidney were waiting for them. Now, Mary Ellen was not the only lady to show off her man. Ida Mae gave Jake a big hug; Mary Sue took J.D.'s hand, and both couples soon disappeared into the crowd.

Having Sidney there really uplifted Rosa Lee's spirit. She had someone special with whom she could enjoy the festival, and she knew exactly when she would tell everyone about Gertie's kind deed.

They would all be having dinner together at a restaurant not far from the festival grounds, and there would be no better time to share the good news. She could hardly wait to see their faces when she told them they would never have to decide about where to have their family reunion ever again. Little did she know that before dinner time, she would have another bit of important news to share.

Sidney was like Rosa Lee had never seen him before. He acted like a teenager taking his first girlfriend to the county fair. He would not let go of Rosa Lee's hand. He led her from one booth to the next. Together, they watched the crafters at work, sampled the food where ever it was offered, and watched the Civil War reenactors.

Sidney even took his turn at the horseshoe tournament. The first shoe he threw fell squarely around the peg. He looked to his companion who gave him a thumbs up. He knew he had impressed his lady with his ability to compete, but his ability rapidly faded. The next shoes didn't come close enough to the peg to be counted which meant he was eliminated. Being eliminated didn't bother him in the least; he'd simply wanted to impress Rosa Lee, and he had achieved what he'd set out to do. Again he'd acted like a teenager.

His next goal was to buy lunch. He located a park bench near the hot dog stand and asked his lady to hold their seat while he got their food. A vendor selling chances on a farm tractor had a booth adjacent to the hot dog stand. A line of people was waiting at each booth. Sidney, not being able to keep his eyes off Rosa Lee, inadvertently got into the wrong line. He was really embarrassed when he ordered two and the vendor gave him a couple raffle tickets. He scribbled his name on the back of the tickets, dropped them in the ticket box, hoping Rosa Lee hadn't seen what he had done. When he saw she was watching him, he just turned red and took his place at the end of the other line.

When at last he returned with their food, she asked, "Are you okay?"

"Not really," he told her, feeling he owed her some sort of explanation "I'm afraid."

"You are kidding, aren't you; what could you possibly be afraid of?"

Sidney placed the food container on the bench beside her and took her hands in his. "I'm afraid you might tell me no, when I ask you to marry me."

Rosa Lee hesitated a brief moment, giving herself time to control her jubilation.

"Judge Duff, are you about to ask me to marry you?"

Sidney knelt down on one knee and removed a diamond ring from his shirt pocket. "Rosa Lee Duncan, will you be my bride?"

Again she hesitated, simply cherishing the moment.

Someone who was as anxious as Sidney for her answer called out. "Say yes, Honey; the gentleman can't hold his breath much longer."

Rosa Lee looked up to see that everyone in the hot dog line was waiting for her answer.

She threw both arms around Sidney's neck. "Yes! Yes! Yes! I thought you were never going to ask. I would be honored to be Mrs. Sidney Duff. The small crowd broke into applause.

When he started to place the ring on her finger, she looked about to see if any of her family was near. When she determined they were not, she asked if they could please wait until dinner time for her to wear the ring.

"Anything you say, dear. Boy, is every one there going to be in for a surprise!"

Rosa Lee's face was beaming as she squeezed his hands. "Make sure you hang onto that diamond sweetheart because you're right; ever one there will be surprised. Let's go find Howard."

"Who?"

"Howard Barton, Ira's chief deputy; he's like family. It just wouldn't be right if he's not there tonight."

The happy couple spent the remainder of the afternoon tasting food, listening to music, watching tournaments and meeting new people. Rosa Lee introduced Sidney to some acquaintances and although she felt like shouting it from the mountain tops, she told no one of their engagement.

They located Howard about half-hour before time for the festival to close. Rosa Lee had no trouble persuading him to join the family for dinner. He could hardly wait to see the expression on the sheriff's face when he learned his mother was the owner of Baxter's farm.

After talking to Howard, Rosa Lee suggested she and Sidney go to the car and rest and just chat for a while.

They had almost reached the exit when a voice came over the loudspeakers. "Get your tickets ready, ladies and gentlemen. We are about to have the drawing for this beautiful new John Deere farm tractor."

"Someone is going to be excited right away," Sidney said. "I looked that baby over, and it sure is a nice machine."

He had barely finished speaking when the voice came over the speaker once more. "Folks we have a winner! The proud owner of this beautiful tractor is Sidney Duff! Remember you do not have to be present to win, but Mr. Duff has not provided any contact information, so if he hasn't come to claim his prize within the next quarter hour we'll draw another ticket." A moment later another call for Mr. Duff echoed through the crowd.

There was no need for a third call because Sidney was there to claim his prize. He thanked the announcer and the dealer who provided the tractor then quickly became hidden in the crowd. When he came back to where Rosa Lee was he asked. "Do you know anyone who might like to purchase a fine looking new tractor?"

"You don't want to sell your tractor, dear. We might use it."

"What in the world can we use a tractor for?"

"We could always ride it when we leave on our honeymoon. Speaking of riding, let's go riding around until time for dinner."

That suited Sidney just to a tee. The festivities were great and much different from anything he was used to, but he wanted to be alone with his new bride-to-be. They drove through the countryside for the better part of two hours. They discussed everything from setting a date for the wedding to where they should live. Rosa Lee listened to every suggestion Sidney made and pretended to be in agreement, but she had plans of her own—plans she could soon make him aware of because it was nearing dinner time.

* * * * * *

Rosa Lee suggested they drive long enough until they would be a little late getting to the diner. She wanted everyone including Howard to be there when they arrived. She also hoped no one who might know members of their family had heard Sidney's proposal.

Her hopes were almost dashed as they entered the diner, for Jake who was seated nearest the entrance was the first to congratulate him. "Yeah," J.D. yelled. "Congratulations. It's not every day a fellow wins a prize as expensive as a new John Deere."

Rosa Lee breathed a sigh of relief. Why of course they knew about his winning the tractor; everyone at the festival had heard the announcement over the loud speakers. She was sure no one there knew about his proposal, or his winning the tractor would have been the second thing talked about.

Sidney, who was as excited as a kid at Christmas, could hardly wait until everyone had placed their order to make his announcement. As soon as the waitress made her exit, he stood, tapped his water glass, and asked for everyone's attention. Their private dining room became silent.

"Before anyone decides to do me harm, I must remind you that I am a judge and there are two police officers present. I have asked Rosa Lee to be my wife, and she has accepted."

Suddenly the dining room was filled with cheers and applause. The hum of congratulatory comments didn't subside until several waitresses appeared with trays filled with food.

Rosa Lee, who was enjoying all the attention she and Sidney were getting was determined to wait until dessert was being served to make an announcement of her own. To everyone's surprise, she stood and asked for silence. 'I know," she began, "there has been much discussion about where we should have our family reunion this year. We all know it would be much too crowded if we were to attempt to have it at Ira and Mary Ellen's home. Therefore I have decided we will have our reunion the same place as always, on the Baxter—I mean the Duncan—farm."

She held the deed in her hand as she asked Howard to stand. "Thanks to my departed friend Gertie and Deputy Howard Barton, what once belonged to Baxter now belongs to me."

There was not a sound in the room, as she asked Deputy Barton to tell the family how all this came about. When he was finished, there was laughter, tears, and shouts of disbelief. Howard, however, set everyone's mind at rest when he told them everything was handled by Gertie's attorney.

"Now," she said to Sidney, "you know what you can do with that tractor."

The celebration lasted for another hour. Sidney and Rosa Lee decided they should get married, on the farm, the day of the reunion. While the others were talking about the upcoming wedding and reunion, Rosa Lee and Sidney were having their own private discussion. When their conversation ended, Rosa Lee made another startling announcement. "Sidney and I have decided we are too old to manage a farm of this size. Therefore, If Ira and

Mary Ellen will agree, we'd like for them and the twins to move back into the farm house and allow us to live in their home."

Everyone except Mary Ellen gathered around Rosa Lee and Sidney, trying in their most humble way to show their appreciation. Mary Ellen sat at the table holding her head in her hands as the tears streamed down her face. When Rosa Lee noticed her, she went to where she was seated. Mary Ellen stood, threw her arms around her and spoke in a voice that was barely above a whisper, "No one in the world has ever been more proud of a mother-in-law than I am of you."

For the next few moments, Sheriff Duncan was speechless. It was hard to tell from his expression if he were overjoyed and so thrilled he wanted to laugh out loud; or if he were so emotional, he was on the verge of tears.

Chapter Twenty-Four

THE WEDDING

The weeks before the wedding were filled with excitement as the Duncan family had never known. With only three weeks before the big day, there was no time to waste. Mary Ellen began moving small items from their home into the big farm house.

Jake and J.D. used the trailer designed for the Green Dragon to move the heavier items and to transport a few personal belongings from Sidney's home in Mt. Airy into Ira's place.

The twins, when not in class, busied themselves using Sidney's new "toy" to finish harvesting the corn left in the field when the Sutters made their unexpected departure.

In a short time, the news of Rosa Lee's good fortune had spread through the community like wild fire through a pine thicket. For some one who was no akin to do such a deed as Gertie had done was unheard of. Folks from all over the county called or came by to see if it was true. Some came to offer their well wishes, and others simply to be nosy. Then, when folks learned she was also getting married to a judge, that was icing on the cake.

Ida Mae begin making her plans for the wedding. She busied herself with such things as making the guest list, ordering the wedding cake, making sure the preacher was going to be available; and, of course, helping the seamstress design the wedding dress.

The members of Rosa Lee's Ladies Quilting Bee insisted they be in charge of the reception. That left Mary Sue to assist her granny with the chore she enjoyed most, spending money. Sidney, who enjoyed shopping second only to digging ditches, gave Rosa Lee a number of signed checks. He gave her permission to purchase anything she felt they might need to start housekeeping. Rosa Lee, being very frugal, made a list of essentials. Mary Sue, who wanted her grandmother to have things she had never before been able to afford, disregarded the term *frugal*. In fact, when she and Rosa Lee finished shopping, J.D. had to make three trips into town with his trailer to haul what they bought.

Rosa Lee wondered if Sidney might cancel their wedding when he saw the sales slip totals. She, however, was pleasantly surprised when he complimented both of them for doing such splendid job.

Sidney spent most of the time in Mt. Airy taking care of legal matters. He'd also made a list of guests he wanted to invite to their wedding.

On a Sunday afternoon, only three days before the big event, everyone in the wedding party was at the farm for rehearsal. Ira, who was to give his mother away, and was about to usher her to where the minister was waiting when the telephone began ringing. A moment later Ida Mae asked her dad to take the call.

"Take a number, Sweetie. Tell whoever it is I'll call them later."

"It's your dispatcher, Dad. He says it's urgent; he must speak to you immediately."

The sheriff had left instructions he was not to be called for any reason so he knew it had to be important.

"Hello. Are you kidding? Tell Howard to take charge; I'll be there right away. Jake will you substitute for me please?"

No one asked what the telephone call was about, but they knew it was of utmost importance to cause him to leave so abruptly.

Sometime near midnight, the family learned why Ira had had to leave in the midst of the rehearsal. Baxter became so distraught learning his farm now belonged to the Duncan family, he had hanged himself in his cell.

"One down, one to go," Jake commented. "Now, what about Patrick?"

"He's waived extradition; he'll be taken back to North Carolina to stand trial. Mom may have to testify; but with all the evidence against him, he'll be gone for a long time."

With the two people who had caused her the most grief out of her life, Rosa Lee hoped the remainder of her days would be filled with contentment.

She could not ask for more. It was Thanksgiving eve, her entire family was coming home to celebrate her marriage to the first love of her life, and she was owner of one of the largest farms in the county. Ira, Mary Ellen, and the twins were once again settled into the spacious farm house. Rosa Lee and Sidney's home was newly furnished and ready for them when they returned from their honeymoon.

John Robert and his fiancé Susan were due at any moment. Rosa Lee and Sidney was entertaining his niece Haley, attorney Bill Wallace his wife Betty, and several other friends who were staying at the hotel in town.

Rosa Lee was being introduced to so many of Sidney's friends she could not remember where they were from or who was married to whom. She didn't concern herself with such trivial matters at the moment; she was sure she would get to know all of them once they were married.

Sidney, Haley, and the Wallaces were the last to leave the farm for the hotel; needless to say, Rosa Lee was exhausted. She took a quick shower and went straight to bed; within minutes she was out like a light. The next thing she was aware of was someone giving instructions about how to arrange something or other. She peered through the narrow slits of her eyelids, hoping she was having a dream. The hands on the Big Ben clock beside her bed showed otherwise. The smell of brewing coffee and the alluring aroma of something she didn't recognize made her realize she should probably get up, but she was still half asleep.

Suddenly, she sat up in bed. She smelled stuffed turkey. It was Thanksgiving, and she was getting married today! She jumped out of bed so quickly her head started swimming. She hesitated a moment before slowly raising the window shade. An unusually warm November morning greeted her.

All the commotion she was hearing was coming from the front yard. Ida Mae was instructing three or four men about how to arrange at least a hundred wooden folding chairs. Mary Sue was helping to place several tables end to end underneath a large tent just below the yard fence. Mary Ellen was covering each table with snow white linens, and someone she'd never seen before placed a huge floral arrangement in the center of each table.

Rosa Lee threw on her robe and made a dash into the dining room. Ira, Jake, John Robert and the twins were making away with large slices of country ham, fried eggs, hash browns, homemade biscuits and gravy. Steaming hot buttered pancakes covered with molasses would be their dessert. They were devouring food so fast one would have thought it was their last meal It didn't take long for her to know why. One of the ladies from her quilting bee rushed from the kitchen and begin gathering their plates, while some of them were still chewing. "Hope you fellers are finished," she said. "We've got to get this place shined up." Rosa Lee couldn't determine if her statement was a request or a command.

Another one of quilting bee ladies shoved a ham biscuit in Rosa Lee's hand and a cup of coffee in the other. "Eat fast," she said. "You have to rush through the shower so we can get you all dolled up for the judge."

Rosa Lee, who had been so busy the evening before she hadn't taken time to eat, was enjoying the ham biscuits so much she thought she might have another. But, as she was about to finish the first, one of the ladies took her by the arm and attempted to help her out of the chair.

"Wait," Rosa Lee said. "What time is the wedding?"

"Three o'clock."

"Are there weddings in Heaven?"

"I don't know, why?"

"Because if I don't have something else to eat, I'll most likely be up there by then."

She did, in fact, have another biscuit, took her shower and then the "get me pretty party" began. The ladies changed her hair style so many times her head was getting sore; but by noon, they'd agreed on a style that suited her best. Rosa Lee added a light dusting of face powder and a gentle touch of pale pink lipstick. She fastened a string of borrowed pearls around her neck and put on the new pastel blue dress she purchased for just this occasion. When she placed the white lace shawl about her shoulders, every one of the ladies agreed she looked as beautiful as a doll in a store window.

As the day wore on, activities on the Duncan farm became more and more hectic. More flowers were being delivered and arranged beautifully everywhere inside and outside the house. Large ribbons and bows were tied on the front-yard fence.

Neighbors from as far away as the county seat begin arriving with gifts and well wishes. Rosa Lee didn't learn until some time later that Mary Ellen and the girls had added friends of their own to the guest list.

No one had seen J.D. and Mary Sue since early morning when they left in J.D.'s pickup. Many of the family members were getting fearful they would not get back in time for the wedding. Their fears were dispelled when they saw J.D.'s pickup turn into the lane about an hour before time for the ceremony to begin. He was towing his enclosed race car trailer which boldly displayed the name, The Green Dragon. He parked the trailer about a hundred yards from the front gate and both he and Mary Sue hurried inside to get dressed.

Mary Sue joined Ida Mae, Susan, and Haley who were the other brides maids, and put on her matching peach colored dress.

Mary Ellen, the matron-of-honor, wore a pastel green dress that blended perfectly with the colors worn by the other members of the wedding party.

The best man, William Wallace, was next to arrive, and he was so nervous one might have thought he was the groom if not for his age. He checked to make sure he had not lost the wedding ring so many times his wife Betty was sure he would wear a hole in his coat pocket.

When J.D. stepped onto the porch, and pretended he could hardly keep his eyes off the beautiful Haley Barber, Mary Sue recalled his reaction to the young lady at the cookout down in Winston, and a jealous streak ran through her quick as a flash. She stepped to his side and whispered, "If you ever expect me to be Mrs. John David Hurd, you best keep your eyes off every pretty lady you see."

J.D. was so joyfully surprised he almost fell off the porch. "Are you asking me to marry you?" he stammered.

"I am, if you will allow me to finish college and continue pursuing my singing career."

"Only if I can continue racing,"

"Do I have to put it in writing?" she said, as the threw her arms around his neck and kissed him like no other gal had done before.

The preacher, whom neither of them knew had arrived, tapped J.D. on the shoulder. "Young man since I am already here, I can perform another ceremony for no additional cost."

This time J.D. did not hesitate, he looked down into Mary Sue's beautiful blue eyes. "What do you say gorgeous?"

"Let me think about it. Yes! yes! yes.! Let's go ask Granny if she and Sidney would mind."

Rosa Lee, who was hidden away, lest the groom should see her before time for the ceremony to begin, was ecstatic when Mary Sue suggested they have a double wedding. Suddenly Mary Sue found she was no longer one of the bridesmaids, but one of the brides.

When the crowd started singing, "For he's a jolly good fellow," Rosa Lee knew her man had arrived. She peeped through the window just as he stepped out of Jake's car. She wondered why he was not driving his own automobile, but she didn't have time to be concerned about that at the moment. It was quarter till three, and she sent Mary Ellen to ask Sidney if the new arrangements were okay. She watched as her daughter-in-law pulled him aside, spoke to him for a moment, then turned toward the window and gave a thumbs up.

Rosa Lee stood staring out the window, feeling so proud to be marrying such a handsome fellow as the judge. Her thoughts were interrupted when J.D. came rushing into the house and asked Ida Mae if he might borrow her wedding ring.

"My what?" Ida Mae asked.

"Your wedding ring. Your sister and I are getting married and I haven't bought her a ring."

Ida Mae hadn't yet heard the news of a double wedding ceremony; but when her granny nodded her approval, she slipped off her ring and gave it to J.D. "Boy are you a cheapie," she mumbled.

At precisely three o'clock, one of the quilting bee ladies started the phonograph and the wedding march filled the air. All the members of the wedding party were in their proper places near the large tent. Every seat was filled and a large number were standing. Kervin and Kevin, who looked absolutely handsome in their rented tuxedoes, were standing on the porch, one on each side of the front door.

When the music began, Kervin opened the door and Rosa Lee with Ira by her side stepped outside. She and Ira walked to the top of the steps and stopped. This time it was Kevin who opened the door. To almost everyone's surprise, Mary Sue and Jake made an appearance.

The men folks escorted the brides to the preacher and the grooms. As if on cue Bingo, Gertie's faithful companion, who was enjoying his new home on the farm, lay down at Rosa Lee's feet.

When the ceremony began the crowd fell silent. It took only about fifteen minutes for each of the couples to say their vows and exchange wedding rings. As soon as the preacher pronounced them man and wife the guests began congratulating both couples.

J.D. whispered to his new bride, "Where did you get this wedding ring?"

"I borrowed Jake's; this one is Ida Mae's, right?"

"They sure are nice. Reckon they would let us keep them?"

Mary Sue just smiled and turned her attention to the well-wishers. Later, they both watched as Rosa Lee opened her wedding gifts, but were not at all envious. They had each other; and for the moment, that was all they needed.

After a couple of hours of enjoying the food and mingling with the guests, it was time to go to the hotel where another party would take place. When Mary Sue suggested she and J.D. not attend, Rosa Lee would have no part of it. Both she and Sidney insisted they would all share in the fun.

"You ladies do whatever you need to do while J.D. and I get our vehicles."

"What vehicles?" Rosa Lee wondered; she'd seen Sidney ride in with Jake. Surely, he didn't intend for all four of them to crowd into J.D.'s old pickup. Be that as it may, she and Mary Sue went inside to check their hair and makeup.

A few minutes later, when they came back onto the porch, what Rosa Lee saw made her begin to cry . Several vehicles were in line waiting to go to the hotel; and in front of the line was a solid black Model-T with Sidney in the drivers seat! The memory of his promise more than half century before came rushing back.

She ran down the steps to the Model-T. She jumped inside, threw her arms around the judge and gave him a long passionate kiss. She would normally have been too bashful to do such a thing in front of all those guests but she was so touched by what her wonderful man had done, she didn't care what anyone else might think.

Behind the judge's Model-T was J.D.'s old pickup with J.D. at the wheel and Mary Sue close by his side. He and his new bride were so much in love they could not have been happier if they had been riding one of Patrick's new Cadillacs. Lots of other vehicles were in line waiting to follow them to the hotel. Ira, Mary Ellen and the twins were in his county cruiser. The sheriff moved to the front of the wedding procession; and with lights flashing, he led the vehicles off the farm and headed for the hotel.

The flashing lights and the Model-T drew the attention of everyone along the entire five mile trip from the farm to the hotel. When the wedding party reached its destination, a bellhop with his head slightly bowed opened the door for Rosa Lee.

"Now isn't that strange, I've never seen a bellboy at this little establishment before," Ira told Mary Ellen.

"May I help you with your luggage, Sir?" The bellboy asked, while never looking up.

"We don't have luggage; we live nearby."

"Then may I park this rattle trap, I mean this whatever it is, for you, sir?"

Sidney was very offended by the comment about his beautiful antique automobile, but he decided to let it pass.

"Is it as old as you are, Sir?" The bellhop asked as he raised his head and looked Sidney square in the eyes and burst out laughing.

"Why, Burley Whitmore! You old son-of-a-gun what brings you here?"

"You, you old moonshiner. I drove all the way from Baltimore to Mt. Airy to visit you and found out you were up here in the mountains. Now that you are retired from the bench, what are folks going to do about all those crooks?"

"Well, I don't know about the big cities, but up here in the mountains they have to beware of "Granny's Justice."

~ The End ~

Other books by James Campbell

Luther's Mule

Ida Mae: Moonshine, Money & Misery

In Her Sister's Shadow

CPSIA information can be obtained
at www.ICGtesting.com
Printed in the USA
FFOW03n0436210917
40216FF